SUCKING DEAD
BOOK 2
MY VAMPIRE BOYFRIEND SUCKS

ANDIE M. LONG

This book is a work of fiction. Names, characters, places, and incidents are either the product of the author's imagination or are used fictitiously, and any resemblance to actual persons, living or dead, events or locales is entirely coincidental.

No part of this book may be reproduced or transmitted in any form or by any means, electronic or mechanical, including photocopying, recording or by any information storage and retrieval system without the written permission of the author, except for the use of brief quotations in a book review.

Copyright © 2021 by Andrea Long.
All rights reserved.
Cover design by Tammy Clarke.
Formatting by Tammy Clarke.
Edited by Andrea Long
Proofread by Mich Feeney

To cupcakes.

Thank you for your delicious existence.

CHAPTER ONE

Lawrie

"Could you please confirm your name?" The shrivel-headed, red-eyed basic bitch asked me.

"Lawrence Alexander Marcus Letwine, formerly Parsons," I said clearly to the seated vampire court.

"And you are aware of why you have been called to this meeting?" she said, adjusting the woollen scarf around her neck. Shame she was already dead. I'd have happily strangled her with it.

"To discuss my siring of a vampire without prior permission, in order to seek retrospective permission."

"Correct. Please be seated."

We were in the boardroom of the Letwine mansion where I had been called for my fate to be discussed and decided. Eleven vampire elders sat in pews in front of an elaborate desk, behind which sat Radaya, the Keeper of the Court.

This was such a faff. Radaya and the elders loved all this pomp and circumstance. First there had to be a ceremonial blood drinking session with a prized blend. They were all dressed in black silk kimono style suits with red robes which made them look like a cult gathered to do karate or some similar martial arts. And after all that, they took forever to get to the point and make a decision. Why I just couldn't say, 'yeah, you got me, I was a naughty boy, slap my hand' and be out of there I did not know. That was the trouble with vampires. Living forever meant new systems didn't come into force like they would in a human world. They still insisted on using an old quill to write all the minutes of the meetings up afterwards, in an old, leather-bound tome for goodness' sake.

I could have been doing much better things... like the hot, blonde delivery woman I'd seen rock up earlier for example. My mouth watered thinking of her delicious human scent. Many a delivery driver had gone home feeling weak at the knees after meeting me. Not just because of my off-the-charts handsome face, but also because I'd had a sweet taste of the fine blood that flowed through their veins.

"Please turn to page two of the prepared report," Radaya addressed the elders and the sound of papers rattling commenced.

"I bring it to your attention that on the eleventh of November, at approximately 11:11 pm, Lawrence drained a Miss Mya Malone, after which he chose to sire her. No permission was sought for this birth. Neither has she been presented before the Letwine Court and advised of her responsibilities, or of the advantages of being a family member."

I managed to turn a snort into seeming as if I had a tickle in my nose. I'd like to see them meet Mya. There was a reason I'd kept her away from here thus far.

"I turn to you now, Lawrence. Could you tell us why you did not follow the Rules of Siring? For anyone who needs it, this can be found in the Original Guide, Page 3276-3281."

"Certainly. I met Death."

There were gasps from the elders, and even Radaya looked startled. This was the problem when your first chance to explain yourself came in an official meeting. "He gave Mya the choice of being made into a vampire and taking the position of Queen of the Wayward in Gnarly Fell, or to be drained by myself and her soul to go to the Field of the Drained. She chose to be Queen and so I had no choice but to sire her. If not, my own undeadness would have been in peril. No one can cheat Death, right? So, there you have it. I went against the rules and sired Mya."

The elders all looked at each other and then at Radaya, who now looked rather flustered as she rustled through the paperwork in front of her.

"The fact remains that Lawrence's continual fraternizing with human females, rather than making use of the blood bank, repeatedly puts him in these situations. I put it to the court that had he not stalked Mya Malone in the lead up to the aforementioned events, we would not be here today," she said, having gathered herself and her paperwork.

Edmond Letwine, the Original Letwine vampire, put up his hand. "I would like to speak to Mya Malone to hear her version of events of the night in question. Right now, we only have the word of Lawrence, who has been known to be economical with the truth on more than one occasion."

Radaya turned to me. "Go collect your daughter."

I whizzed through the ether, appearing where Mya's scent called out to me like my own. *Family.*

Then I brought her back to the court. She stood in front of everyone, her hair mussed and pulled her blouse back together hastily. She glared at me. "Could you not see I was *busy*, Dad?"

Yes, I'd seen she was busy. It was why I'd called out, 'Sorry, family meeting' to Death, whose hands had been on the buttons of the blouse. It was a good job I'd formed a strange, tentative friendship with the guy because he'd not looked very happy. Then again, the guy was moody and broody most of the damn time from what I'd seen.

"Good evening, Mya Letwine, formerly known as Malone."

Mya placed her hands on her hips. "Good evening, Ms who-the-fuck-are-you, and it's still Malone for your information."

Radaya's face paled further if that was at all possible and the red of her eyes glowed.

"Could you please keep your daughter in check, Lawrence?"

"Could I just have a private, five-minute conversation with my daughter outside? She wasn't expecting to be brought here today and so I would appreciate being able to prepare her for a court appearance."

"Very well," Radaya said.

I quickly whizzed myself and Mya outside the building.

Her hands went to the wall as she tried to steady herself, before she turned around and glared at me *again*. "Stop doing that or I'm going to call down to the basement and ask the keeper of hell if he can spell you to an immortal time loop of feeling like you've been punched in the nuts."

"Mya," I implored. "I don't have long. Drop the bitch-strop. I need to give you a quick rundown of the Vampire Court and why you're here."

She sighed. A long, bored, dramatic sigh. "Do you not think I've had enough to learn lately? You know, all about death. And I actually mean death as in dying, not Death as in Big D and the bedroom."

If she didn't shut up soon, I was going to go back in the courtroom and ask to be placed in the Field of the Drained for some peace and quiet.

"Mya. I am on trial today for siring you without advanced permission which is a big no-no. They've just heard my defence that I was given no choice by Death and your decision to become Queen."

Mya's mouth dropped and the drama escalated to Oscar and Bafta levels, with dramatic hand movements and pacing. "You didn't have a choice? Oh, but meeeeee, I could choose between being drained to your stupid field of nothingness or being made a vampire. Poor you, boohoo."

"We're ready for you to come back now." A court clerk stood outside, raising a brow at me. Clearly, he'd heard how far I'd got with 'talking' to Mya.

"Please behave. You are my firstborn and I need you to be an example of how great I am at being a sire."

"Let's go," she huffed. "The sooner this is over, the sooner I can get back to business."

"Do you think of anything but sex?"

"Not really. It puts me off the fact my new best friend is..." Mya put a hand over her mouth.

"Dreary? I gather you're talking about Callie?"

"The court are getting irritated," the clerk advised, so I whizzed us back inside, whatever Mya's reply was getting lost in the breeze.

"Good evening, Mya. Please take the seat we have placed at the top of the room next to your sire," Edmond directed. "I am Edmond Letwine, the Original of the Letwine vampires. I would like to officially welcome you to the family."

"Thank you," she replied politely. I would have breathed a sigh of relief if I breathed at all.

"So, Mya," Radaya looked upon her. "I am Radaya, the Keeper of the Court. I am a Breedent, which means when vampires first descended it was from my family. They bore the first set of vampires. My line commenced the Letwine clan."

"So you're his mum?" Mya asked, staring across at Edmond.

"We don't do the whole mum and son thing in the vampire world; everyone sired is family," Radaya clarified.

She looked at Edmond. "My parents sucked too, just not via a jugular."

I closed my eyes at that point, waiting for Edmond to stake her and take my firstborn off the family tree. Instead, I heard a giant belly laugh.

Radaya called everyone back to order. "Could you please tell us what happened the night of your siring please, Mya?"

"Of course," Mya said, sounding almost chirpy which made me feel uneasy. "So the person previously known as Hottie," she pointed at me, "came into the bookstore where I worked and asked me on a date. He then, unbeknown to me, the rat bastard, daydreamed about my being his evening dinner.

Except Death turned up and got in the way of his plans. I chose to be Queen, given the alternative was to lie on your field of fuck all, and so Daddy had to turn me. The End. Wow, what a literary feast my story is. I might send the idea to a publisher. It's no more freaky than Hansel and Gretel is it?" Mya looked from Radaya to Edmond.

"This corroborates the story from Lawrence. We will now retire to chambers to discuss our decision," Edmond said. "Thank you, Radaya, as always."

She nodded and disappeared.

"Mya, I do hope you will consider coming for dinner sometime soon so we can get to know you better," Edmond asked her, which startled me as he rarely entertained anyone, bored of the whole new vampire thing after so many millennia.

She smiled. "I'd like that. Can I bring my boyfriend with me, if he's free?"

"Well, that's not usually the way we do things, but..."

"No. Absolutely not," I protested.

"And your authority here is?" Edmond bellowed.

"Yes, what is your authority here, Daddy?" Mya tilted her head to one side and laughed.

I placed a hand across my chest, lowering my gaze at Edmond as if I was sorry. "My apologies, sir, for talking beyond my place. I'm sure Death would love to come visit." It killed me to not grin after.

"Death? Your boyfriend is Death?" Edmond's voice went a few octaves higher.

"Why does everyone react like that?" Mya replied, but the slight smirk to her upper lip showed she knew exactly what she was doing.

She curtsied of all things to Edmond. "I shall call you grandfather as you are the grand-father of them all. Let me know when I can visit for dinner. I'll bring my dad instead. Personally, I think that's a fate worse than Death, but hey ho."

And then she was gone.

An hour later the Vampire Court reassembled. I'd waited around the grounds until they'd finished debating my future.

Now Davinia, one of the elder female vampires, stood to give the court's decision.

"Lawrence Alexander Marcus Letwine. The Court have hereby decided that on the count of siring Mya Malone, you were not availed of acceptable alternative options, and we therefore retrospectively grant permission for her siring."

"Thank you," I answered, rising from my seat ready to leave.

She raised a hand. "I have not finished speaking. Kindly refrain from talking until you have been given permission to do so and sit back down."

Oops. Edmond didn't let her talk much, so she wasn't going to be happy I'd interrupted her. I retook my seat.

"We are all agreed however that the fact remains you were put in this position by your constant frequenting of London. Therefore, for the remainder of 2011 you are only allowed to travel to Gnarly Fell where your daughter resides, and otherwise must remain at the Letwine mansion."

I was soooo desperate to talk right now. If talk meant protesting vociferously.

"We also think it is time you found an official consort. You can find your own amongst the female vampires of the mansion or we can assign one to you."

There was a pause.

"Now you may speak. Do you accept our conditions?"

But for once I was actually speechless and so could only nod my head in response.

CHAPTER TWO

Callie

"I love Christmas and I can't wait for Christmas Day," I told Mya, followed by a happy sigh. I couldn't help it. I'd always loved the seasons and Gnarly Fell at Christmastime was truly magical with us being such a small, intimate group of villagers.

Staring at the newly filled counter of the cupcake café I owned, I smiled. Along with my usual cupcakes were home-baked mince pies and gingerbread Father Christmases. I'd done some special flavoured cupcakes this year: advocaat angel cakes, all pale buttercream and gold sprinkles with fairy-cake style wings, wrapped in lace-style cases; and elderflower elves, with green icing and shiny red balls (behave yourself, I know where your mind went), stripy cases and candy-cane legs. Over the past few days, they'd been selling like hot cakes, which I guess they were when they first left the oven. My friend though was sitting at the table across from me snacking on her usual red velvet, having arrived before I officially opened for the day.

"Enjoying it?" I waggled my brows. Only a select few knew about the extra ingredient in my 'special edition' red velvet... O-neg.

"Always." Mya smacked her lips together.

"So, come on then, aren't you excited for Christmas? I mean it's your first in Gnarly and your first with your new boyfriend. Don't tell me you still haven't made plans yet."

She shrugged. "There are still a couple of weeks yet, so I think we should make the most of every single day and every single minute. Is there anything you've always wanted to do? Like a bucket list type of thing?"

I wrinkled up my nose at her suggestion. "I don't believe in that garbage," I replied. Mya was acting strangely today and given she was a vampire who dated Death himself as well as being the Queen of Wayward Souls, that took some doing for her to act even weirder than normal. We'd been friends since she'd come to live in Gnarly in November, which meant we'd known each other around a month now. She'd been a breath of fresh air when she'd arrived; ironic given that taking her last breath was the reason she now lived in the castle on top of the hill, just outside the gates of Gnarly Fell village.

It was thanks to Mya that the curse on our village had been lifted. A curse that had hovered over the village for years that had meant no resident had been able to enjoy a happy ever after. Now the witch who'd created the curse was living her own happy ever after in Mya's castle and was allowing us the opportunity to find ours.

"What don't you believe in? Living every day like it's your last, or bucket lists?"

"Bucket lists. You should live every day like it's your last anyway."

"Yeah, you're right there. If I'd have known I was going to die, I'd have bought more pairs of Louboutins on my last shopping trip." Mya lifted up a black patent shoe and rotated her ankle to show off the red sole. "At least Big D allowed me to go back to rob my old apartment."

"That wasn't my recollection of events." I lifted a brow.

She rolled her eyes. "He should have known what I meant when I asked if I could visit one last time to make peace with leaving my old life. I felt much more peaceful once I was reacquainted with my shoes."

"Couldn't you just have ordered a new pair?"

"No, because everyone here is all about reusing and recycling. I'd never hear the last of it from Milly and Tilly if I bought something new just for fashion." She mock shuddered. "And I don't want to get on their bad side; the weirdo-twins might haunt me in my sleep."

"You are so cruel about those two. They've just lived a sheltered life that's all. The second-hand shop has been passed down through the generations. You never know, now the curse has been lifted, maybe they'll start dating and become more independent from one another. I know, I for one, can't wait to start dating now there's a chance of a happy ever after."

Mya emitted another heavy sigh. "I think you should hold off on dating. What's the rush after all this time? I'd let Christmas get out of the way. Busy time at the café, right?"

"Okay. You're being beyond weird. What's going on?"

"Nothing." Mya played with the now redundant cupcake wrapper.

"Oh, I get it," I said, folding my arms across my chest.

'Y- you do?"

"I'm totally forgetting that Death might not be around for Christmas. He might have to go out and collect souls, right? I mean, it'll be in The Book of the Dead, won't it? Are you wanting to spend Christmas Day with me and Dela? Is that it? You should have just asked."

"You got me there. Yes, there's a death in the book that he'll need to attend, although it's all rather up in the air as just occasionally destiny will change and the person's death either changes or disappears from the book. Like mine for instance. Originally it said that Lawrie would drain me, but then Death made it that although he would drain me, I'd come here instead of the Field of the Drained. So it might be that the person doesn't die and then everything will be okay."

"Mya, quit rambling. You can have an open invitation to mine. If Death's around it's fine for you to stay with him up at the big house. If you're at a loose end, come to ours."

"So how is your sister anyway? Still swiping right like she's a windscreen wiper in heavy rain?"

I grinned at her joke. "Yep. Dela is determined to

find her beloved before I find mine. She said she's sick of always being second, being the younger one. I might strangle her though, if she keeps slacking off her shifts due to hangovers and last-minute dates. She can be the first to die then. Hahahahaha. Hey, see if it's in your book that I finish her off." I laughed, but Mya didn't laugh back.

"Mya, I'm only joking for goodness' sake. I'm not really going to kill her."

"Oh, I know. Ignore me. You're right. I am in a weird mood today. I guess it's just that this is my first Christmas here and we just met, and we seem like we're going to be the best of friends and..."

Mya started to cry. A weird sight given the dilute red that ran down her face. I moved my chair around to hers and hugged her, then passed her a clean napkin from the table so she could wipe her eyes. "Oh, sweetie. Christmas is always an emotional time. I know you said your family were shitheads, but I guess you're feeling the loss of your old life and what you used to do. It'll be okay. We're all here for you, babe."

She sniffled while wafting her hand in front of her face trying to calm herself.

"And we are going to be the best of friends. And one day, when I finally get my happy ever after and get married, I'm going to make you dress up in a pink bridesmaid dress and if Death hasn't married you by then, I'll throw you my bouquet and wink at him."

Mya's tears became hysterical sobbing. I was getting concerned now.

"What is it? Is it the pink? Or is it marrying Death? I mean living together is perfectly acceptable, you don't have to catch the bouquet."

Mya was trying to get a handle on herself and waved me off. "It's nothing. I'm fine, really. Do you have another napkin or tissue?"

Standing up, I walked to the counter and returned with a handful of napkins, noting it was nine am and my first customers were opening the door. "Here. I'm sorry you're feeling so rubbish, but I need to go see to my customers now. I'll be back when I can." I gave Mya an arm squeeze, but she jumped up.

"I'll j- just pop to the b- bathroom," she said, escaping through the door at the rear that led to the customer toilets.

Mya's peculiar behaviour had both mystified me and unnerved me. Did vampires still have a time of the month? Surely not? Lawrie had told me it was rare for a vampire child to be conceived and born naturally and that 99.9% of the time they were sired through the vampire's turning of them. Pregnancies were an anomaly with more chance of winning the lottery.

Ugh, Lawrie. Why did I have to think of that utter dickhead now? Lawrence Letwine, vampire, and the man I'd mistakenly once accepted a date with. The less I reflected on that, the better. Luckily, some more customers walked in and then I was too busy to revisit my past disaster.

Mya eventually walked out of the bathrooms looking good as new. I shouted over to her. "Go sit in the corner and when things get a little less busy, or my sister finally gets her backside out of bed, I'll bring us fresh drinks and we can discuss what the book club read should be for over Christmas. I know people choose their own books now, but I always get the Karen Swan Christmas book and save it for Christmas Day. We could suggest that we all read the same one just this once?"

"Yes. That. Absolutely that," Mya answered both emphatically and determined. "But not to save it for Christmas Day, to read now, to get us all in the festive mood."

"Ooh, okay, I can do that."

Maybe Mya was a Karen Swan fan too? She seemed very keen for us to read it.

A couple of customers got up to leave, nodding goodbye to me, and so now I had a table I needed to clear. "Well, that was sorted quickly, so if you have other plans, don't let me keep you."

She shook her head. "No, I have no other plans. I just want to spend time with my new best friend. I can help you serve if you like?"

"Erm, no, that's okay. You have to be trained and I've no time for that." A queue was already forming now due to me talking to Mya instead of serving. At that point my younger sister made an appearance, her strawberry blonde hair swept off her face in a bun, ready to put her cap on. Her pale, freckled complexion looked a tad on the green side.

"Okay, I must get on. Dela doesn't look like she's going to be much use."

After taking my place back behind the counter and giving Dela a large dose of side-eye, I took my next customer's order and accordingly set the coffee machine to pour an Americano with an extra shot. Before it had even finished filling the cup, Dela swept it up and took a huge sip. "Fuck, that's hot. Aargh, my tongue."

"It's also Fenella's," I snapped, turning to look at the woman who ran the local laundry service.

Fenella giggled. "Serves you right, Dela. Good night, was it?"

"No," Dela huffed. "I thought the curse was lifted, but I'm just dating arseholes."

"Maybe go for the whole body next time?" I quipped.

"And that's why you're single." Dela gave me a look of derision.

"I'll find someone. If death is written in a book, then my thinking is that love might also be written in one. Maybe Cupid holds it?"

"Maybe you need to stop reading those stupid romance books and switch to murder mysteries. Cupid. As if he's real."

"So Santa lives in Gnarly Fell, but Cupid doesn't exist? Is that what you're saying, because that makes no sense." I'd not wanted to argue with Dela this morning, but I was already annoyed she'd been late for her shift and now she was pissing on my potential love bonfire.

"That's exactly what I'm saying, and Stan A is not Santa. How many more times? The letters of his name also spell Satan. So your reasoning is stupid because he could therefore also be the devil."

I finished serving the slew of customers and then

told Dela she could handle the next thirty minutes on her own while I took a break and sat with Mya.

My friend gave me a half-smile as I walked up with two fresh drinks and placed them on the table.

"I've ordered the Christmas books, so that's all set," she told me.

I took the seat across from her. "You should start the same tradition as me, if you enjoy the book. We could both make it a best friend forever thing to read Karen's new book at Christmastime."

Mya's waterworks threatened to start again.

"What is it now?" I asked.

"Y- you said best friend forever."

I tilted my head and made an awwww face. "Well, I'm hoping you are."

"B- but that's the thing. Oh God, he said I shouldn't tell you, but maybe we can change it."

"Change what?"

"Th- The Book of the D- Dead." Mya could barely get her words out, but I felt my face drain of all colour as I realised what was coming before the words were uttered.

"It says you'll d- die on Ch- Christmas Eve."

CHAPTER THREE

Lawrie

A consort?

A woman to be glued to my side forever more. Basically, a splinter never to be rid of seeing as vampires lived for an eternity. Someone who might start off fabulous like a majestic tree, only for my hands to splay down that fine form until the time the splinter got under my skin, hurting and itching and needing to be removed desperately.

No thanks. Lawrie Letwine liked to be alone.

Free to choose a different new flavour every night. I much preferred to sample all the different species than be stuck with one of my own and the blood bank. If that was my new fate I may as well let someone shove a stake through me now.

At that point Callie Francis' face came unbidden

into my mind. The owner of Callie's Cupcakes in Gnarly Fell hated my guts and would gladly do the deed if I went and took her a stake. In fact, I bet she'd saw down the front door of her beloved café in order to oblige.

I shook my head trying to dislodge her image from my brain. Our date had been an unmitigated disaster; something I still didn't fully understand given women loved me. Actually, she could stake me using the big stick she carried up her arse.

I wandered around the grounds of the mansion while I sulked over my punishment. It wasn't my fault death made me sire Mya, so why should I now have to settle down? I reckoned the elders had been just looking for an excuse to bring me in line and this was it.

"My dear friend, what ails you? I've never seen you look so... tense." The voice of my friend Bernard—pronounced *Berrrrnaaarrrrd* unless you were Death or Mya—echoed from behind me. I paused my stomping around until he reached my side.

"It was D-day, and I'm not happy with their decision," I replied through gritted teeth.

"I can tell. Your teeth are clenched and so are your buttocks, *mon amie*."

"How. Many. More. Times? You are not French."

"I was drained in the Eiffel Tower bathroom on a romantic getaway, as you well know. Don't take your pissy mood out on me."

"Sorry."

"Pas de problème."

My fangs descended.

"Mon dieu! Okay, okay. I'll speak bloody boring English like I have for my entire two thousand years of existence. Forgive me if I just enjoyed speaking a different language for a while so I didn't faceplant through tedium."

It was a given side effect of being a vampire that from time to time we got extremely bored. We just had so many years to do things, try things, that sometimes it got too much. When we felt like we might walk into a sharp tree branch, we visited our physicians who gave us a tincture that let us sleep for a few years. The rest did a vampire good, and that was where the myth about vampires sleeping in coffins had come from, because when they took respite, they did sleep in a coffin. It was the only place they could be sure as to not be disturbed.

"Sorry. Again. One hundred years can be tedious, never mind two-thousand."

"Apology accepted. So, what happened in there?"

"I got the retrospective siring permission, but…" I sighed. "I'm banished to here and Gnarly until after Christmas, and…" I swallowed deeply. "They want to find me a consort."

I watched as the corners of Bernard's mouth twitched, then it spread across his face, until he creased over with mirth. The next thing I knew he was laid on his side, holding his stomach and laughing hysterically. I kicked him, hard.

"Ooomph."

"Get up and come to the bar with me. I need a stiff drink. It's the only thing that will be stiff in my life from here on out if I have to take a vampire wife."

Bernard flew to his feet, knocking dirt and grass off his dark trousers and pale grey t-shirt with his long fingers.

"My wife is a vampire and I have no problems getting stiff at all. She is utter perfection."

"But don't you get bored with her?" I asked as we walked back towards the house, ready to head to the building behind it: The Vampire's In(n). It had been named long ago by a vampire with a sense of humour who liked the fact they didn't have to be invited over the threshold given it was on vampire ground. The whole invite thing was a nuisance, but you only had to be invited once and for that reason vampires regularly used the same haunts outside of their home.

"No. I never get bored. Aria is the most perfect thing to walk the earth."

"You're lucky then if you still think that after all this time."

Bernard pointed to his ears.

"What's wrong with your ears?"

"For a supposedly intelligent man you have zero common sense." Aria appeared before us, all long, curly red hair and green eyes. "He's miming that I can hear what he says due to my vampire hearing and should he not say I was the most perfect thing to walk the earth, he should find himself enjoying anal via the nearest fence post."

"Ahhhhh. Now all becomes clear."

"But, despite the fact we have been together years, he still does make my heart go flippety-flop."

"You don't have a beating heart," I said.

"I'm speaking metaphorically. And we shall now have to find the person who makes your heart metaphorically flippety-flop also. Like for instance, you should go on a date with Katerina. Then we could double date."

"Absolutely not. She looks like a toad."

"You have to stop basing all of your decisions on looks. Katerina is an incredible woman and she assures me that wide mouth of hers has extra talents."

"I would wager she's eaten more than just a man's penis," I scoffed.

"Lawrence. That's enough. You have got to see beyond the façade. For instance, you are a very attractive man..."

I preened and ran a hand through my hair.

"...but a complete obnoxious arsehole."

"God, you sound like Callie."

"Callie Francis," Bernard sang her name. "The one that got deep under your skin because she didn't fall for your charms. You've never got over that, have you?"

"She just turns my stomach every time I think of her. Terrible woman."

"So terrible, you begged her for a date, what was it... eleven times?"

"Ferme la bouche."

"No, I will not shut my mouth. You fancied her, begged her for a date, and you just have never been able to understand why she wasn't interested."

"Of course I don't understand. It's me! How can

any woman not be interested? I am the whole package." I started my explanation even though Bernard and Aria had heard it all before. "I'm beautiful, educated, can satisfy their every desire in the bedroom, and then I respect their need for time to themselves, the whole 'me-time' thing."

"'Me-time' does not mean you go let someone give you a blow job, Lawrie," Aria scolded.

"Women want things all their own way. My 'me-time' is having a woman blow me while I do nothing at all. Just take time for myself. Then you go back to your date and get called a cheating scumbag. Do I get annoyed that they used the shower head when they could have had my head between their legs? No. So why can't I have my dick sucked? Am I supposed to pull the bath plug out and see if the pull of the vortex sucks me off? Btw it doesn't."

Aria's arms were crossed over her chest and the fingertips of her right hand drummed her left arm indicating she was getting pissed off with me. "So how come you can go to Gnarly Fell and you aren't just grounded to the mansion?"

"Because of Mya being my daughter. I'm allowed to visit family. Though why would I want to go to Dreary Fell... The women there make Katerina look like Miss World. Some of them are pretty, but they are the strangest people. Anyway, being Mya's father, I have to attempt to teach her about Letwine vampires. Edmond seemed especially taken with her for some reason."

Bernard raised a brow. "Our leader took an interest in a fledgling? Interesting."

"He liked her sass, it would appear. Thank God, or she'd not have survived the introduction."

"She certainly has that. Though I shall stake her myself if she doesn't start to pronounce my name correctly." Bernard was clearly still affronted at Mya's English pronunciation.

"Let it go. She's doing it on behalf of her boyfriend and you know it. She's happy with Death; you're happy with Aria. Let that one lie."

"I suppose I could. It's not like I have to see her often, if at all."

"I'm glad he's found himself someone," Aria said, and then they were both gone.

Looked like jealousy meant Aria was in for a damn good evening.

Meanwhile, I now had no drinking buddy. But that wouldn't stop me. I pushed open the doors of The Vampire's In(n). I needed a great deal of scotch to get through the night while I tried to work out how I got myself out of this mess.

"Lawrie!" The heavily bosomed barmaid Ginny greeted me with a warm, familiar smile. Which she would given she was my 'sister' and I'd given her the money for the boobs. Although we were one big clan, whoever sired us meant we kind of had siblings and Virginia was mine. My sister wished to be a kept woman and hated her job behind the bar, saying she only did it as it tended to be visiting vampires' first port of call and she wanted first dibs on any rich, attractive ones, male or female. My sister swung in whatever direction their bank accounts laid. Our 'sire' had met his maker a long time ago, so I kept an eye on her when I could. She was probably the only thing I cared about, and I didn't make it obvious because caring was a weakness in our world and led to danger. She knew I looked out for her, and she also knew I didn't advertise it. The situation worked in reverse too.

"So I heard you have to take a consort. Poor bitch."

"Yeah, well, I pity the person that ever ends up with you. The only vampire who drains bank accounts instead of blood supplies."

"Go screw yourself."

"If I could, life would be so much easier, dear sister."

She poured me a scotch and placed it on the table. "First one's on the house," she said.

I raised my glass up to her. "Cheers."

I got the feeling eyes were watching me and I looked around to see various female vampires staring at me like I was on a menu as that night's special.

"Just give me the bottle," I instructed my sister. "I'll take it to my room." I couldn't afford to get drunk here and let any of these women get their fangs stuck into me.

I needed a plan fast on how to survive the next couple of weeks.

The scotch went down as smooth as my tongue along a waxed snatch, but it made me maudlin and before I knew it, I'd started drunk dialling.

"What?" Bernard snapped.

"What am I going to dooooo? All the vamp bitches were thhirrrsstyyy tonight. You get me?"

"Just a minute. Aria says she has an idea. Two secs."

Aria's voice came on the line. "I've been reading a romance book. It's called Fake Fiancée."

"That's very interesting, but I'm having a crisis here so can we do book club another night?'

"God, you are so dumb. That's what you need. A fake fiancée. Go find someone you can put up with and make them a deal, like pay them or something. Then everyone leaves you alone. It gives you some time to figure things out."

"Aria. You, my girl, are a fucking genius," I announced. "If only you were not already taken."

"Well, she is, and if you don't mind, I was busy showing her just how much."

The line went dead, but I didn't care because now I had a plan.

A fake girlfriend. My plan didn't get any further because at that point I passed out.

CHAPTER FOUR

Callie

I laughed. Yes, that was my response at being told I was going to die. That's when I realised there were so many different laughs in the world.

My laugh of disbelief.

Mya's laugh-come-huff of confusion at my response.

The giggles in the café from people enjoying themselves while they enjoyed my cupcakes because they obviously hadn't just been told they were *going, to, goddamn, die.*

I noticed that Mya was staring at me, waiting... and then I was suddenly in the middle of the woods as I screamed hysterically before a bout of dizziness meant I fell on the floor clutching at my head.

"Sorry, but I couldn't let you scream like that in your café."

I looked up at where I felt Mya's voice had come from while I waited for the world to settle and be still once more. Feeling something strange, I picked at my hair dislodging a small twig.

"Whereas me disappearing won't alarm anyone at all," I replied with vehement sarcasm.

"Oh yeah. Just a moment," she said before disappearing again.

I laid back and stared at the sky and at the clouds while tears built at the corners of my eyes before running down and off my cheeks.

I was going to die?

In two weeks' time?

But I had so much left to do on earth...

I didn't have a steady boyfriend. I had never been married. I had no children. I'd never been to Edinburgh where I'd always wanted to visit. I had never tried Scuba diving. Okay, that's because I didn't like putting my head under water, but still... there was so much I hadn't done with my life.

Mya re-appeared.

"All sorted. There were only two humans who'd been invited to the café, and I did my power of suggestion thing on them. Everyone else was perfectly okay with us whizzing off."

I sat up and hutched backwards, so my back was resting against a tree. Mya came to sit next to me.

I turned my head to face her. "Mya. Am I really going to die?"

She sighed and tilted her head. "I hope not, but the book does say so." She shot up as if zapped by a cattle prod. "Then again, I died and then was undead so maybe I can have a word with Lawrie and get him to sire you too?" Her words were coming out crazy fast, such was her hope and excitement. "You know how he'd love you calling him Daddy."

"Fae can't be turned into vampires."

She slumped back against her own tree trunk. "Oh. Well that really sucks."

"Yup."

My mind was just in a vortex of thoughts: Primarily, *I'm going to die*, mixed with all the things I hadn't yet done. I was twenty-eight for goodness' sake.

"What the hell am I going to do, Mya?"

"Well, look. I could be staked at any moment, so although you have your death predicted, mine could also come up, as could anyone else's, so all you can do... all we all can do... is live every day like it's our last anyway."

"You're right." I scrabbled up onto my feet. "I need to get home. Can you take me straight back?"

A crease appeared between her brows. "Err, I think we should wait a little longer. You've a lot to process. You only found out you were going to die six minutes ago."

"Mya, I need to shave every hair off my body and get out to a club and bag myself a stud muffin. If I'm going to die it's going to be courtesy of my heart packing in from too many orgasms."

She shook her head. "I've already told you that you need to be careful. Though it's hard to stop death in its tracks, it's not impossible. However, getting it to come quicker because you've changed the course of events for yourself is not sensible, so you can't really be going out picking up strangers and bringing them home, or even worse going back to theirs." Mya scrubbed a hand through her hair. "I just don't see a way around this except me being your bodyguard until the book changes its forecast."

I slumped back down to the floor. "You can't do that. You have a whole undead new life to be enjoying."

"Of course I can. You're my new best friend and

I need to keep you alive. I've eons of time to be undead probably."

She pulled me in close for a hug and though I was grateful for the comfort, she'd forgotten how strong she now was with her new vampire strength and was almost suffocating me in her bosom.

I made a series of gasping noises before she realised. She was just letting me go as I noted a shimmer in the air and then Lawrence 'loser' Letwine appeared in front of us.

"The only thing that could make my current situation worse and here he is." I huffed. "What do you want?"

He licked his top lip. "To watch, if you two are having a little make-out session while hiding in the woods. Do carry on. You won't even know I'm here."

I folded my arms across my chest. "Don't be ridiculous. She's giving me a hug as I'm having a very bad day. What are you doing here anyway?"

He sneered at me, looking down at me from his standing height to my sitting position. "What's happened? Did a tray of cupcakes burn? You've no idea what a bad day is. Try being turned or facing the vampire court. Anyway, not that it's any of your business but I came to see my daughter."

I moved my attention to my friend. "While the

loser is right and it's not my business, Mya. I think it's only right to point out that the only reason Lawrie would come to see you is if he needs something. It certainly won't be to your advantage or because he gives a damn."

Mya was looking from one of us to the other like she was at Wimbledon watching the ball volley back and forth.

"So what happened after I left yesterday?" she asked him.

He leant against a tree. "Oh, nothing much. A little telling off, that's all. Anyway, I thought we could hang and maybe sneak off out of Gnarly, do something exciting. What do you say, oh daughter of mine? My treat."

She smirked at him, and I saw his face fall. I was suddenly a lot more interested in this conversation.

"But, Daddy, you're not allowed out of Gnarly, are you? Unless of course you're staying at the mansion, so where is it you think I should sneak you off to, bearing in mind I could get in trouble with Grandpa for doing so?"

"Grandpa. *Grandpa?* It was grandfather yesterday."

"Yes, well, Grandpa decided to give me a call this morning to let me know the results of your hearing and to forewarn me that you could only be in Gnarly Fell or at the main house until after Christmas."

"That goddamn man."

"He's amazing. He has the full measure of you. He also told me your other news."

Lawrie gave an imperceptible shake of the head, but I saw it. Oh my, I was so invested in Lawrie's shit show I'd forgotten for a moment that I was going to die.

"So who's going to be your beautiful bride?"

"You're getting married?" My mouth fell open.

"No, I most certainly am not." He flicked his hair. "Not a chance."

"But Grandpa said you have to find a consort. That they're fed up with your behaviour and you have to settle down."

Lawrie's face looked like he'd just had his head in an extremely yucky-filled nappy or had to taste someone else's vomit. How happy it made me was clearly an issue I should be raising with a psychologist.

So happy that despite my imminent demise, I laughed. Hard.

One minute Lawrie was leaning against the tree, the next he had moved, grabbed me by my shirt, and now I was being pushed up against the tree. Closing the space between us, I could feel the bark of the tree against the back of my neck and through my t-shirt. Face not a hair's breadth from mine, he snarled as he looked down on me, fangs descended. Mya flew to our side, but I held up my hand. I wasn't scared of Lawrie.

He sniffed at my neck, running his nose up and down the skin from the bottom of my ear to my collarbone. I felt my skin goosebump, but I kept my chin tilted upward and met his sneer with a look of sheer defiance.

"My life is basically over because I have to settle down and you think this is amusing? That shows just how selfish you are," he growled out.

"It's always about you, isn't it, Lawrence? Your life's over. You can't date and annoy women anymore. You can't understand why I don't find you attractive. It's because you talk about yourself allll niggghhttt long. You. You. You. You. You."

"You're such a bitch. Suck a dick and die."

I turned to Mya, looking through the small space between our heads. "Is that how it happens, Mya, on Christmas Eve? Do I suck a dick and die? Because if so, that's not so bad really. At least I'll be enjoying myself. Unlike now, where the precious moments of my remaining life are being WASTED BY THIS TOSSPOT."

Lawrie hissed slightly. I knew he hated shouting. It hurt his super-hearing ears. Hah!

Mya chewed on her bottom lip for a moment before finally speaking. "I know I can't tell you what happens, but I'm sure Death won't mind me saying that it's not from sucking a dick. Not at the moment anyway, because like I said things change and if you start picking up random strangers and shagging them, then who knows."

Lawrie dropped his hold on my shirt and turned to look from me to Mya. "What are you talking about, daughter?"

I pushed him, though of course being both an irritating and a strong vampire he didn't move. "I'm dying. On Christmas Eve. It's in The Book of the Dead. So you'll be rid of me soon enough and at least when I'm dead that means no you, so it has its plus points."

"Dead? Fully dead? Buried dead? Like, never coming back dead?" he asked, his finger tapping against his lip when he'd finished talking.

"Yes, so you can have a party. They do a funeral pyre for us tooth fairies so you can come roast a marshmallow as you say good riddance."

"I'm trying to stop it," Mya informed him. "I have no idea how, but I need to stop it. She can't die. She's my best friend and I need her. So I'm going to stay with her. Be her bodyguard."

"No, you're not. I told you already that you need to go be with Death and the wayward. That's your role and you're only just learning the ropes."

"How did you know... *oh,* you mean metaphorically," she said.

Lawrie removed his tapping finger from his lip and placed his fingers and thumb to cup his chin. "You need a bodyguard?" Lawrie double checked. "Twenty-four-seven company, to make sure no one offs you?"

"No," I said.

At the same time as Mya said, "Yes."

"Well, well, well. You see, right now I need something too."

I rolled my eyes in anticipation of whatever sarcasm was about to be emitted.

"I need a fake girlfriend. Now ideally, I need one until the end of the year, but if I manage to thwart those who want to kill you either altogether or at least until December 31st when I'll be free again, you would do. In fact, the more I think about it, the more perfect it is, because I can't stand you and you hate me. Therefore, watching you pretend to love me would be quite entertaining throughout the two week dullfest I have ahead."

My mouth dropped open because I was sure I'd just heard Lawrie say he wanted me to be his fake girlfriend in exchange for keeping me alive until the end of the year. Hysteria about my death sentence was clearly alive and well and in the building. I'd better go get some sedatives to help myself calm down.

"I know you can't stand my dad, but that is actually a really sweet deal," Mya said.

"You can't be serious!" I gasped. "I'd have to move Dela out and him in. And I'd have to spend time with him. My last two weeks on earth, spent with this narcissist."

Lawrie made a choking noise in his throat. "I'm not a narcissist. Everyone is always getting at me saying nasty things when all I ever do is try to help. Really, people should be sympathetic to me. I've had it hard, ever since..."

I broke a loose hanging branch off the tree and attempted to aim it at his chest, but he grabbed my wrist. "Steady on there, *girlfriend*."

"I'm not your..."

Then I sighed. A very loud, very audible sigh.

Because I knew if I didn't say yes, Mya would stick around, and I didn't want that. I also knew that Lawrie might actually be able to save me from a would-be attacker. He didn't need to sleep for very long each day, and he was super strong, super fast, could read human minds and make them do his bidding, had superior hearing and eyesight and was trained to drain.

Lawrie saw in my face I'd come to this conclusion and a smug grin came over his features before he laughed. Hard. Letting me have a taste of my own medicine from earlier.

"I need a drink. A really strong drink," I said. The fact it wasn't ten am yet not putting me off in the slightest.

CHAPTER FIVE

Lawrie

"Let's go back to the café and talk about this properly," Mya said. "Because in my opinion, it's likely one of you will die at the hands of the other if this is agreed."

"That is acceptable to me."

Callie shot me a look of malicious intent.

"I meant going to the café, not our demise," I stated. "I will be able to have a delicious cupcake while we ponder the final details, like whether or not we share a bed." I watched Callie's reaction to my words, and she did not disappoint.

Her nose had wrinkled up, and her lip curled. "You barely need to sleep so you'll be on the couch. Or Dela's room at a push if she allows it."

"But how will I be able to protect you properly if

I am not by your side twenty-four-seven?" I made puppy-dog eyes and batted my lashes at her.

"I think I'll just accept I'm going to die, Mya," Callie said, making me guffaw.

"I'm messing with you. Let us do what Mya says and go to your café and discuss this further. Come to an agreement that suits us both."

Callie nodded reluctantly and Mya grabbed her, told her to hold on tight and we whizzed back. I, of course, appeared straight back in the main shop, but the other two didn't.

Dela startled. "Lawrie. Jesus, man. What have we told you about not doing that? Since the curse lifted, more humans are visiting the fell due to us all now being able to date and potentially find our happy ever afters. They aren't going to return if they see people appearing out of thin air. They'll go visit the doctor instead."

"How comfortable is your bed?" I asked her.

She slapped me straight across the face.

"How dare you. You permanently pester my sister because you can't believe she doesn't want you, and now you have the cheek to appear at my counter and try it on with me. You're despicable."

"I *am* despicable. I'm the epitome of the bad boy persona. Do you know writers write bad boys based on me and readers flock to read them? It makes women wet, Dela. Soaking wet. However, I am not the slightest bit interested in you. Something about you does not appeal to me."

She slapped me again.

"Goodness, Dela. Make up your mind. Are you annoyed you think I'm making a pass at you or annoyed that I don't want to make a pass at you?"

"What do you want, Lawrie, other than me sticking the coffee stirrers together to make one big stake and serving you that?"

At that point, Mya and Callie walked through from the back. Callie looked very peaky and I recalled a previous period of vampiric travel when she'd been the same.

"There you are," Dela said. "I'm dead on my feet. It's been chaos here running the place single-handedly."

"Hey, that's something I'll be able to help with, darling," I said to Callie, who turned even peakier.

"I need to sit down," she said. "Sorry, Dela, but you'll have to carry on a little longer, only we have things to discuss."

Dela folded her arms across her chest. "What's going on?"

"I'm here to save the day, Dela," I declared.

"I'll tell you shortly," Callie said. "It's been quite the day and I really haven't got my head around everything yet, but please be patient. What's happening is urgent. That's all I can say right now."

"Fine. But I want tomorrow off. I have a hot date tonight."

"Deal," Callie said. "Now, what does everyone want? I'll bring it over to the back table."

"Shouldn't we go upstairs to discuss such delicate matters?" I asked. "You never know who is listening."

Callie sighed. "I guess so. Jesus, it's just I said you would never, ever be invited upstairs."

I smirked. "And I told you I would."

Five years earlier...

Despite being alive for years it was incredible how you forgot places existed or was yet to discover them. I'd smelled the most incredible aroma permeating the air as I whizzed through to the centre of London and so I circled back, landing in Gnarly Fell. I remembered the place from old. It was full of supernaturals, but cursed. However, I'd never smelled such a delicious scent before that wasn't from someone's veins.

I followed the smell and stood outside the place named Callie's Cupcakes, standing in the open doorway.

The first thing I did was wince. The place was pink. Fifty Shades of Fucking Pink. It looked like someone had binged Angel Delight and spewed it around the place. Despite the intoxicating smell, I was just about to retreat when I spotted the most delicious morsel.

The waitress.

Pink-haired, about which I wasn't surprised. Dressed in a tight, fifties-style dress, also pink, with a white apron, she looked and smelled like one of her concoctions.

She looked over at me and smiled. "Hello and welcome. Are you going to come inside?"

"May I?"

"Of course. That's usually how I serve people." She laughed.

I walked inside and up to the counter.

"So how may I help you today?"

Moving nearer, I took a deep inhale through my nose. A perfect O-neg, complimented by a sweetness from eating lots of sugar. She was clearly fae, her deli-

cate freckles in their particular way of lying on her face told me that. But what kind I wasn't sure.

"I'm at your mercy, as I'm intoxicated by the aromas that have brought me into your café but find myself spoiled for choice."

"I have the perfect answer for that. I do a selection plate. A drink and three small cupcakes: chocolate, strawberry, and vanilla. Unfortunately, I don't stock your drink of choice and it's not available fresh from this source."

I smiled, beguiled by her sass. "I've already fed today, so a lemonade would be perfectly acceptable to go with your delicious sweet treats. And a date. You intrigue me..." I raised my brows in question.

"Callie. The clue is in the name of the shop."

"You weren't necessarily the owner."

"I'm wearing a name badge."

My eyes flitted to her dress. "I should get brownie points for not looking at your boobs where I see that badge is situated."

"That's because your eyes have moved from my face, to the cupcakes, to my neck."

"I like you." I smiled. "You're feisty, and you smell irresistible."

"Well, I'm not available, but if you go sit down the cupcakes are."

It took me another ten visits to the shop before Callie gave up and agreed to come on a date with me.

"Oh my god. Okay. You're driving me insane. Fine. One date. Where do you want to go? It has to be somewhere very public as I'm not any of the meal choices."

We agreed on a meal at an Italian restaurant with an outside dining area. I had never been so enamoured of a date before. There was just one thing perplexing me. Although I picked up a vibe that she quite liked me, my vampire allure did not seem to be effective around her. I couldn't make her like me.

Which just made me want her all the more.

"Is this public enough for you?" I asked Callie, just after we'd been seated in the central area of the al-fresco dining section.

"Yes, thank you. Great choice of restaurant too if the TripAdvisor reviews are anything to go on."

Callie looked sensational in a sleek, black dress that fit every curve. It had a large pink sash around the waist, and I couldn't help but think she'd dressed up as a present for me. Clearly, she liked me more than she was letting on and if I was lucky later, I might get a tasty nip. And I didn't mean her bosom's stiff peak in my mouth.

"So, I know you have just recently opened the café

and you were born in Gnarly Fell, but what sort of fae are you?"

She took a drink of her rose wine. "So you worked out I was fae?"

"Your freckles give it away."

She touched her face. "My mother always made me cover them up, but I like them. She said it gave away our secrets."

"You should never cover them up, they're adorable."

The meal progressed amazingly. We had so much to talk about and fell into a natural banter, quite unbecoming of a vampire and a fae who tended to stick with their own species. And then everything started to go awry.

A woman came up to the table. Just stood there staring at me.

"Can we help you?" Callie said, at which point the woman pushed Callie and her chair away from the table, grabbed another chair and sat opposite me staring into my eyes.

"What the hell?" Callie said, getting up from the chair.

"Lawrie is mine," the woman said without even turning her head away from me. Her blank stare was unnerving.

"How do you know my name?" I asked her.

"Do you not remember me?" The woman said, tears now pouring down her face. "You told me I was special. You said we had a connection. I let you... b- b- bite me."

I sprung up, my mouth falling open, and I looked at Callie. "This is impossible. I vampire brainwash them afterwards. Something must have gone wrong. Give me a moment."

But then over the woman's shoulder, I saw the door to the café open and five more women walked in heading in our direction. What was happening here?

Callie turned in the direction of my horrified gaze. A queue of women were now at the door.

She turned back to me. "Lawrie. What's going on?"

"I don't know. It must be my allure. Somehow it's attracting every human female around."

The voices all started at once, like some ethereal chorus.

"Lawrie."

"Lawrence."

"Lover."

"Lawrie."

"Why did you take me and leave me?"

The waiter came bounding up. "Er, could you control your company, or ask them to leave. They are causing a disturbance."

"Yes, of course." I started my vampire mojo. Looking intently, one by one, into the eyes of the women around me. "You will remember nothing. I don't care for you. I never did. You will leave here and return to your home and forget all about me."

The women started to turn to walk out of the building and that's when I saw Imelda, a vampire I'd dated and dumped as soon as Callie had agreed to come on a date with me. She'd allured my human dates, the ones who I'd taken out previously to get a fresh sample from. She laughed from outside of the window and walked off, with a final middle-fingered salute. I knew she was unhinged. Clearly, she'd been stalking me after I'd ditched her. Still, I'd take stalking over staking any day.

"I am so very sorry about that. Bitter ex," I told Callie.

But she was shaking her head at me, her eyes flashing venom, not the understanding I was now expecting. "Un-fucking-believable. You've led on countless human women in order to sample their goods in more ways than one, and when a vampire one decides to serve you a course of revenge, you blame her."

"No, that's not how it is," I said, while thinking it was exactly how it was.

"I'm going home." Callie threw some money down on the table. *"That will cover my share."*

"No. Callie. Please don't leave. I really like you."

"If I asked every one of those women, would they say you told them you liked them too?"

"I don't know. I don't care about any of those women."

"Well, aren't you just a delight, Lawrence Letwine."

"I didn't mean it like that."

"Could you order me a taxi, please?" Callie called out to the waiter.

"I can but there will be an hour's wait at least."

She looked at me like you might look at a runny dog turd you still have to attempt to pick up because there's a person behind you watching what you're doing.

"Would you please have the grace to take me home?"

"Of course." I sighed.

We walked outside and I whizzed her back.

Callie went extremely dizzy. "Oh God, I think I might throw up."

"It will settle. You just need some water." I went into her fridge situated behind the counter and brought her a bottle out. Handing it to her, I watched her take a few sips. Slowly, her face lost its green tinge, though she'd still looked cute as green went fantastic with pink.

"Can you stop looking at me like I'm supper?" Callie yelled.

"I'm not. I'm just thinking you look cute."

"I've just almost been sick. How is that cute?"

"I think this date got off on the wrong foot. Can you please remember that although I'm a vampire who has in the past sought blood direct from the source, I can avail of blood banks. I'm extremely attractive, wealthy, and it really wouldn't be in your best interests for you to call it quits at this stage."

Her jaw dropped. "Have you heard yourself?"

"Of course. I have superior hearing, you silly sausage. Look, if you're feeling a little better shall we take this upstairs? We can talk some more, and I'll explain about the whole ex-dates thing. There's no need to feel threatened."

'GET OUT."

I winced. "Can I politely remind you of the superior hearing thing?"

"I SAID, OUT."

I'd had my hands over my ears that time just in case. "Can I not come up just for five minutes and you hear me out? I am a lovely man and would make an amazing boyfriend."

She prodded my chest with her index finger. "Let's get something VERY clear here. You will NEVER, EVER, be invited upstairs to my home. You're a conceited jerk. Now get out because I have a megaphone upstairs from when I helped out at Gnarly's recent sports day and I'm not afraid to use it."

I held up a hand.

"Okay, okay. But just know that I shall keep visiting, and I won't give up."

"Please yourself."

"Oh I will, as soon as I get home, while I think of your face and those perfect rosebud lips."

I whizzed off out of there, happy to have had the final word that evening.

From then on, my pursuing of Callie turned from wanting another date, to starting to resent the one woman who didn't want me. Before long, tormenting her had become my favourite pastime.

And hating me had seemed to become hers.

CHAPTER SIX

Callie

This could not be happening.

If dying wasn't bad enough, being murdered was the icing on the cupcake. Then having to live with Lawrence Letwine was the sprinkles on top of the cupcake of death.

Typically, I then started imagining the ingredients for such a cupcake, thinking of Death himself as inspiration. Totally needed to be chocolate, but then it needed a shock centre, maybe a soft strawberry as Death had revealed his soft side to Mya.

I turned to her. "When you think of your boyfriend, do you ever think of strawberries?"

She pulled a face. "No. I think of his enormous cock."

I managed to refrain from asking her what it tasted like—just.

Dela's expression was just as confused as the three of us passed her to go upstairs to the apartment above the cafe that I shared with her. As I approached the bottom of the stairs, I hesitated and turned to Lawrie.

"I suppose I'd better invite you upstairs officially."

He shook his head, a smirk starting to sneak over his face. "No need. When I was invited into the cafe, you then invited me in to the whole building."

I gasped. "So you could have come upstairs at any time?"

He smirked. "Indeed. So do I get some gold stars on my reward chart for the fact I never did?"

I sighed, knowing that I would spend a lot of time between now and the date of my death doing that.

We reached the top of the stairs and I opened and walked through the door at the top which revealed a narrow corridor from which off-shot the two bedrooms, bathroom, kitchen, and living room. The whole thing was cosy, and it was a good job Dela and I got along well as a rule. Now I would be getting cosy with the man I detested more than most others.

But at least you might get to live, so that's the sacrifice you must make, my inner voice chided, sounding very much like Mya. I then realised my mind guard was down and it *was* Mya giving me her advice via her thoughts.

"Quit that," I whispered.

Lawrie sat himself on my sofa, lounging against the back rest, all long limbs sprawled in front of him, his arm resting on the arm of the sofa. "There is no point whispering, darling; superior hearing, remember?"

I sat down next to him and beckoned him to bring his head nearer.

He laughed. "I'm not falling for that again, and if you still have that megaphone, I will use my superior strength to crush it."

I made an attempt to move myself, but he tugged me back down. "Oh no. I think I like you there, by my side. It's the perfect place to discuss our 'arrangement'." He said it like we were going to have some kind of sex pact and then my mind decided to go off on yet another tangent. One where I had hot and dirty hate sex with the idiot at my side. Thank God my mind barriers were firmly in place because if he'd got any hint as to the X-rated show that had just trotted through my brain, I would have thrown myself straight out of the window.

"So does anyone want a drink?" I asked.

"Nope. Mya doesn't want one either. We're vampires. So stop making excuses to try to get away from me. The sooner you realise this is just how it's going to be for a while, the faster we can get on with the plan. Shall I start?"

Mya took a seat opposite us in the armchair. "I will be the chairperson of this meeting. If I ask either of you to be quiet, you will listen."

We both nodded.

"Okay, Dad, you're up first. What do you need Callie to do?"

Lawrie spoke while looking mainly at me, although occasionally he turned his head towards Mya. I had managed to shuffle myself up to the other end of the sofa. It was only a two-seater so I was still nearer to my enemy than I would have liked, but it would have to suffice.

"I don't know how much you know about this, Calliope, but..."

I held up a hand to interrupt him. "My name is not Calliope."

"Hmm, I felt sure Callie was the shortened version of that. My apologies Calpurnia."

"That's not my name either."

"What is it then?"

"Calendula."

Lawrie snorted. "Calendula? As in Pot Marigold? Oh my, please can I call you Marigold?"

"No, you can call me Callie, or I can cut out your tongue."

"Is Dela a shortened name too?" Mya asked, taking us completely off what we were supposed to be discussing.

"Yes, it's short for Delphinium. A lot of our family were named for flowers. As you can imagine, we didn't want to have to utter such a mouthful every time we wanted to speak to each other."

"Yes, you need your mouth empty for other things." Lawrie winked.

"God, I hate you." I narrowed my eyes to tiny slits at him.

"Your eyes remind me. I do love a tight slit," he whispered.

Mya clapped her hands in front of us. "Okay, let's focus on why we are here. Lawrie, please continue."

"I found myself at the vampire court due to my

siring of Mya without permission. Of course, I had little choice given Death made me do it, but I still had to face the elders. Luckily, they granted me permission and backdated it. However, they also decided that I had to seek a consort and that my general behaviour was not satisfactory. My friend gave me the idea to have a 'fake' relationship. Someone I could present to my family and friends, while at the same time doing whatever the hell I still liked, albeit further afield so the rumours didn't reach my family."

I opened my mouth to speak, but he held up a hand.

"However, I shall refrain from dating others if you agree to my filling the position of bodyguard until either when you die or after the new year, whichever comes first. I will just need you to convince my family that I am not a cad, but a delightful and lovely person who should be allowed to choose his own love should things not work out. I.e., if you expire or we fake break up."

"So I would have to come meet the family?"

"Of course. And keep up your mind shields because they will try to read you and that would be a disaster."

"But in return you will be my security detail,

ensuring that no one gets to try to kill me?"

"Absolutely. I will be by your side. Even helping out in the cupcake cafe. I'll be with you in the shower, while you sleep, when you get dressed..."

"Lawrie, stop it," Mya interrupted.

"Why does everyone always want to spoil my fun?" he complained. "So, my little Marigold. What say you?"

I folded my arms across my chest.

"I agree to you being my bodyguard. The other details we'll have to thrash out, my little penis."

Mya cackled.

"I shall call you Callie from now on, if you could call me Lawrie," the suitably chastened vampire at my side announced.

"Aww, I was quite taken with *mon petit pénis*."

Mya called us to order. "Okay, so we have an agreement that for at least until Christmas Eve you will assist each other in these matters."

Mya's phone rang, and she broke off her conversation to answer it.

"On my way." She ended the call. "Duty calls. I have to go. New wayward incoming. Call me later if you need me. Bye." With that she was gone. Suddenly, I felt very vulnerable.

"So tell me, what happens to fairies when they

die? It's something we have never been told," Lawrie asked and this time there was no snark or mirth to his tone, which made me look at him closely. Was Lawrie actually capable of being serious? Who knew?

"If we are born in the mortal realm, we just return to the earth. And both myself and Dela were born here, in the woodland of Gnarly Fell. There's no rebirth, or afterlife in the Otherworld for us. We just end."

"And the only things that can kill you are steel or iron?"

"Yes."

"Okay. If you think of anything else that will help me protect you, let me know. I need to return to the Letwine Mansion to gather some belongings. Would you like to accompany me, so you won't be alone?"

I shook my head. "I've only just found out I'm going to die. I could use having the rest of the day to myself and then I need to tell Dela everything. The book says I should be okay until Christmas Eve and I'm sure Mya would let me know if it changed. So, if you could come by later? I could phone you?"

"Okay. I will await your call."

He rose from the sofa, ready to depart.

"I know it's not much consolation, but I didn't get any advance notice of my own death. One moment I was human, the next a vampire. At least if you only have two weeks left on earth, you know to make the most of those two weeks, right?"

"I guess so. Thanks, Lawrie." It was the first time I'd been halfway civil to him in a *very* long time.

"Mon petit pénis is available at short notice should you desire it," he said. I took a step forward ready to slap him, but with a giggle he was gone.

Bastard.

When he'd gone, I laid down on the sofa and thought about everything I'd been told and that had happened. I cried, I got angry, I became determined to beat my murderer. I wondered about who it could be. Whether Mya had made a mistake. My sister had become increasingly angry about how busy the shop was, wanting to come up and see what was wrong with me. I wouldn't let her close early. No way was I letting my customers down. Bad news could wait.

Eventually Dela came upstairs looking worn out. She wasn't one for hard work and today she'd had to do some. As I went to get her a bowl of hot water for her tired feet, she threw herself onto the sofa with a groan. "I am dead on my feet, sis. Dead. Now before I fall asleep, which could be in the next few seconds, tell me what is going on."

"Let me just get you a foot soak."

"No point, my eyes are already closing, so come on. Have you been secretly shagging Lawrie? I knew you two couldn't be passing all that verbal foreplay between you all the time without boning."

"I'm going to die, Dela."

She sat up, no longer looking as tired.

"What?" Her brow creased and she stared as if she'd misheard and was waiting for me to repeat myself with something like 'I'm going to make a pie'.

"I'm going to die. It's in The Book of the Dead. I die on Christmas Eve. Mya wasn't supposed to tell me, but she did. I don't know how it happens."

"Bullshit," Dela spat. "You are not dying. Over my own dead body."

"It's why Lawrie was here. He's going to be my bodyguard. I'm going to do everything in my power to change the course of The Book of the Dead's forecast, but I have to accept I might not be able to."

Dela broke down in noisy sobs and we spent a long time talking about what I knew, what we could possibly do.

"I'm not moving out," Dela wiped at her eyes. "We'll just have to make it work, because I need to spend as much time with my sister as possible if you might..." her voice cracked, "die."

"Okay. We'll figure it out," I said.

"You need to tell me everything you've always wanted to do, but haven't done yet, and we'll make a bucket list."

"What is everyone's fascination with these lists? I don't need one. Also, I don't want you to tell anyone else in Gnarly, okay?" My eyes fixed on my sister's face and her expression told me she knew I was being deadly serious.

"Okay. I won't. I promise."

"Thanks. I want to spend my time doing all the things I love in Gnarly, like going to book club and running my café."

"Surely you want to do more than that if you're going to die? Don't you want to visit New York or anything?"

"No. I don't think I do." I sucked on my bottom lip. "Maybe this is just shock speaking. I'm sure I'll have plenty of emotions to work through yet. But right now, I just want to be as normal as possible. We just need to keep a close eye out for my potential murderer."

"I will feel better with Lawrie here to protect you," Dela said. "I'm desperately tired now, which annoys me because I don't want to sleep. I want to spend every available second with you."

"I know, but that's just not realistic, Del. Anyway, you get ready for bed." I remembered she was supposed to be going out then. "What about your date?"

"I'm cancelling it. I'm far too tired."

"Sorry, I spoiled your date making you work all day."

"Like I give a shit about that now."

"I'm going to text Lawrie now and let him know he can return if he's ready."

"I slapped him earlier."

Dela told me about how she'd slapped him twice in the café. We laughed and then she went to her room after giving me a hug that lasted so long, I had to shake her off me. I knew she was crying as she left, but I was running on empty myself now. I needed to sleep.

I sent Lawrie a text and within thirty seconds he appeared right in the living room in front of the sofa.

"You look tired. Let's hit the sack," he said. "Lead the way to the bedroom, hunny bunny."

CHAPTER SEVEN

Lawrie

I might have sounded confident, but to be honest I was a little out of my depth, because Callie was unpredictable. Most women I could wrap around my little finger, especially the human ones. What I didn't manage from the thrall, I usually managed via my charm. So to be in Callie's apartment, having agreed to move in to bodyguard her... well, it had all happened super-fast and I felt a bit like I'd had a dream and not quite woken up yet.

"I'm not going anywhere yet," Callie told me with that feisty look on her face, chin raised, eyes sparking like they might combust. I felt my cock harden. "We need to discuss this 'situation' further."

I looked down at my trouser area. "I can't help it.

It's a natural reaction, and when you get all cocky, so do I."

"Lawrie, I am not talking about your cock. I'm saying that we need to discuss us living together more. About what we're going to tell people about the fact we're suddenly in love when everyone knows I hate your guts."

I slumped onto the sofa. Callie once again moved right over to the other side.

"Very well. Let's sit here awhile and discuss all this and then you need to sleep."

She tugged at her ear. "While I sleep, what will you do?"

I shrugged my shoulders. "Not thought about it. Maybe a crossword or two. Binge read something on my Kindle. I know you fae ordinarily age slowly and live for hundreds of years, so you must realise that as an immortal being, time isn't really anything special to me. Because I have so much of it. Such a manmade construct means little to my kind. If I wasn't keeping an eye on you, I could whizz off to the Caribbean or something and be back by the time daylight appeared."

"And you were turned in the 1920's?"

"Yes. I've been around for over a hundred years. Turned when I was twenty-nine."

"I haven't experienced any longevity yet. I've aged like a human so far. Usually we 'freeze' at around thirty and then age extremely slowly from then on. If we're not due to be murdered that is."

"Why are you insisting on sitting so far away from me on the sofa? You do realise that from tomorrow we'll be having to hug and kiss and things, so you doing that is pointless?"

"Let me enjoy myself while I still can, I beg you," she said dramatically.

I rolled my eyes. "If there was a prize for sarcasm you would most certainly be the recipient it was awarded to."

There was silence for a moment and then Callie spoke again. "How did it go at the mansion? Did you tell them anything or did you just say you were staying at Gnarly for the night?"

I thought back on my few hours at the mansion and recounted the tale to my new fake girlfriend.

A few hours earlier...

"Ah, Lawrie," Edmond appeared in the giant sitting room where I'd placed myself knowing he would find me. The guy was clearly on a mission now

they'd decided I needed a consort. "I thought we could have a little chat."

"Yes, indeed, Edmond. I have some news to share with you. Something I have decided to come clean about."

Suspicion hung off the elder's face. He'd seen too much in his time, and vampires trying to get out of his orders were nothing new. I knew I needed to tread carefully.

He perched on the arm of the sofa, giving him the height advantage. Liked a good psychological manoeuvre did Edmond. "Sounds intriguing. Please enlighten me."

"I have been dating a fae lady on-and-off for several years. When I told her about how you wanted me to take a consort, she immediately told me she loved me and that there was to be no more shilly-shallying between us. That we were to make our commitment one way or another. We therefore decided that we were committed to our relationship, and so I have no need of a consort."

"So you're engaged? Lawrie, I have to say that is a surprise, but congratulations."

"Erm, no, no we're not—"

"Oh. I thought you said you were committed to the relationship? If it's just dating, I don't see why

you still can't meet some of the vampire women I have in mind for you."

"—not officially engaged. Please allow me to finish my sentence," I said, while inside my stomach felt like I'd swallowed a rat. No, I was just looking at one. Edmond was playing me, but I had no choice but to be played. Otherwise, it was vampire consort time.

"Go on. I'm all ears."

"We only discussed this earlier today. I told her I wished to propose properly, and so until that time we are planning to become officially engaged, but at the moment it's just something we know we want. I came here to tell you and to ask for your approval for bringing a fae into the Letwine family."

Jeez. I was making this shit up as I went along and seemingly re-digging the grave I rose from approximately ninety years ago.

"I wish to meet her first, before you propose officially. If she gets my seal of approval, then I will agree to this arrangement and remove the need for you to take a vampire consort. She can come to dinner tomorrow evening. Bring your daughter too. Does Mya know this lady given she's from the fell?"

"Yes, sir. Mya is friends with Callie."

"Callie? The Callie I hear hates your guts? This is your soon-to-be fiancée?"

"You know what they say, Edmond, that there's a fine line between love and hate, and Callie and I love to hate each other at times. It's why we've been on-and-off so much. However, faced with losing me, Callie decided she couldn't let me go. We shall be able to talk more upon it tomorrow evening at dinner."

In other words, please let me stop talking now, because I might say something even worse that resulted in a bloody wedding. Actually, if it took place on Christmas Eve when Callie was due to be murdered it could be!

Edmond cleared his throat, unimpressed that I'd stopped concentrating on him.

"Eight pm in the banqueting hall. If Mya needs to bring her boyfriend with her, get her to ask him to refrain from wearing his cloak."

"Okay. I'll see you tomorrow. Just to add, sir, if I may, that I will now be living with Callie in her apartment at Gnarly Fell until we've had further discussions about our future, given she runs the cupcake café. I intend to help her with her business for a while."

Edmond wobbled on the chair arm. "You are going to serve cupcakes? A mighty vampire is going to work in a café? I forbid it."

"It's a cover for the fact I want to keep a close eye

on her. You know women these days. They don't get all the old-fashioned protector idea. They think they don't need us. I intend to save her from some predicament until she realises she can't live without me... literally."

"Lawrie, you've always been a little... unpredictable, shall we say? But right now, I'm tempted to call on Dr Murgtoff to check you over."

"Why? Because I'm in love with a fae? If I wished to be by the side of a vampire consort would you be questioning my motives? I hope you're not being discriminatory towards the fae there. Love is love."

"Of course not. Oh, just be here at eight tomorrow, Lawrence." With that he whooshed off. I always had had the knack of pissing him off to the extreme.

And now I just had to return to Gnarly to tell my new ward that not only did she have to come for dinner and an interrogation, but that I needed to propose.

◊

"Absolutely not. No, *no, no, no,* NO."

"But he's expecting us."

"Not no to the dinner, dummy. No to you proposing."

"Is it not on your list of things to do before you die?"

"I'm not doing a list, and no, being proposed to by Lawrence Letwine would not be on it."

"You wound me."

"Please excuse me while I just visit the bathroom for a moment. I need time to think."

"You can say you need a number two. Everyone poops."

She screamed then. It hurt my ears. Then she stomped off.

I looked around the place that was due to be home for a couple of weeks. It was very small indeed. Not helped by the fact that in one corner of the cramped living space was a large Christmas tree, festooned with the most amateur and vulgar ornaments. Like a piece of eggbox sprayed silver, and a fat Santa. Stan was actually built like a rugby player. I wondered what he thought about the fact he was always portrayed as portly.

An odour emanated from the couch. I'd not noticed it while Callie sat there as the notes from her perfume tickled my nostrils instead, but now the whiff took hold. I began lifting up the sofa cushions, eventually finding a rotting apple core. I would have to clean this place. That was one thing I could do tonight while she was asleep. I could clean super-fast thanks to my vamp speed and get this place to smell a whole lot better.

Callie walked back in after some minutes. "I did not poo," she announced.

"Oh I know."

"What do you mean?"

I pointed to my nose. "I'd be able to smell it. Also, if you fart, it will assault my senses. I'll get accustomed to it though quickly, so all is good."

"All is far from good," she growled out. "So let me get this straight. Tomorrow evening, I have to meet the main Letwine vampire, the elder. The one person who can probably burrow into my mind and find out the truth. And I have to convince this man that I want to marry you?"

"Yup."

She pulled on the hair on the top of her head. "Is this worth it? Maybe I should just face up to the fact I'm going to die and just live my best life until that happens."

I pulled her into my arms and held on tight until she gave in, smooshed against me. "No, Callie. Meeting the vampire elder is not as bad as being dead. That's what you have to remember. No matter what my life is like as a vampire, it trumps my demise."

"Tell me about your turning," she said. "I need to think about something else for a while."

"Okay," I acquiesced. It had been a long time since I'd gone into the details of my turning. I'd briefly told Mya how I'd been sired, but I knew right then Callie needed a distraction. So distract her I would.

"It was nineteen twenty-one..." I began.

CHAPTER EIGHT

Callie

I was wrapped in Lawrie's arms. Well, more like trapped because he was insisting on what I guessed he imagined was comfort. In reality it was like being a fly in a spider web, with the web threatening to break your bones as it wrapped around you.

"C- can I just interrupt you to ask you to loosen your hold a bit, or I might need the orthopaedic ward of the hospital shortly."

He loosened his hold, but annoyingly didn't let me move. Now just imagine for a moment you are shopping in the chilled section of the supermarket. That's what being next to Lawrie was like. Lawrie thought he was cool, and he bloody well was. If he was going to keep cuddling me, I'd need some thick jumpers.

Then he began to speak, and I was so interested, I forgot I was cold.

"Times were of course very different back then. They call it the roaring twenties, but life could be hard. My parents had been looking forward to me moving out and making my own way in life. I was betrothed to Elizabeth, and we were due to be married that following month. Then I lost my job. Elizabeth had been insisting on various fineries I couldn't afford for her bridal trousseau, and I stole some potatoes from the farm I'd been working on. I'd been caught and rather than have me arrested they just told me to leave.

"It wasn't a life Elizabeth wanted, one married to someone who had no employment. I'd said we'd have to postpone the wedding. Within a week she ended our relationship for a man who drove a Buick and worked in a bank.

"I had no money, no fiancée, my parents still wanted me out of the house, and then the rumour broke about my being a thief. I guessed another farm-hand, who'd never liked me, had decided to tell Elizabeth's new partner, Ted. Ted was determined to not look like the bad party in all of this drama surrounding her ending our relationship and starting afresh with him, so it would make sense having been him who spread it. My parents threw me out as I'd brought shame on them."

"So where did you go?" I asked, invested in the story of how Lawrence went from scorned boyfriend to arsehole vampire.

"I took myself to a bridge near the river and decided there was nothing else for me to do but throw myself over and let the currents take me. But while I was there mulling over the best place to aim for, where the stones were more jagged or might knock me unconscious as I fell on them, an extremely finely dressed gentleman appeared seemingly out of nowhere. I just thought I'd been so busy contemplating my suicide that I'd not noticed him approach."

"But actually he was a vampire?"

"Yes. William Letwine."

At this point, Lawrie began slowly running his fingers up and down my arm. I was about to protest when I realised he was unaware of it, doing it while he went back in time to tell his story. Maybe it was a comfort thing? I knew I didn't want him to stop telling his tale yet, so I just let the matter go, trying not to accept the fact it felt quite nice. As I looked up at Lawrie, I saw he was completely lost to the past. His gaze inward, unfocused. It was hard to equate the Lawrie I knew to the man whose life had turned so dismal he'd wanted out of it.

"William was very gentle in his approach, asking me if I was okay, because he sensed I wasn't, and I didn't know what it was, but he really seemed to understand. I found myself telling this man my whole tale. Of course, swiftly after my turning I realised it was because he had me in his thrall. I told him everything. How I'd lost my job, my fiancée, my home, and he asked if I wanted to join his family business. I'd never want for money again. I'd have a lovely home, whatever partner I desired. He said I had nothing to lose but to try and that I could always walk back down to the river another day, so I said yes. The next thing I knew I was under that bridge with my life being drained out of me and then I found myself a fledgling vampire."

"I'm guessing that's tough. Mya's told me a little about her early thirst and how she almost went on a drinking spree."

"William was ruthless. I'd told him my story and so he took me, hungry, straight around to Ted's house. He was home alone and in no time, I wasn't as hungry, and Elizabeth once again found herself with no future husband. With him dead and me now missing, it was surmised that I had killed him in an act of jealousy and revenge and then run."

"So you never saw your parents again?"

"Only from a distance. And at first as you watch those you love age and then die while you stay the same, it hurts. But as the years pass and you don't have any of those emotional attachments you become harder. Humans became food sources. No different to how my parents would kill farm animals. It's not personal, not now. Not really. Although as you know, I delight in being a bastard and getting the upper hand. Got to get my fun somewhere. Many things bore me after all this time."

I yawned.

"Am I now boring you?"

"No, I'm just tired. It's getting late. It's been a very long, very exhausting day, finding out I'm going to die. Then you've moved in, and I'm beat. I need to be up early to open the café, so I'm going to make a move. You okay here on the sofa?"

"I am. I will however need to use the bathroom after you. I still have a night-time routine."

"Okay."

I moved off the sofa and got ready almost automatically. I was so tired I fell onto my bed. Not even the terror of my upcoming murder could stop my eyes from closing.

However, not long after I fell asleep, a large thumping on my bedroom door followed by it opening, did wake me up.

I found Dela standing in the doorway.

"Can you get this twat out of the bathroom? He's been in there for thirty-five minutes."

I rubbed at my eyes. "Is he having a bath or something?"

Lawrie appeared in the doorway. "I am done in there now, Dela." She huffed and stormed off in the direction of the bathroom.

"I told her I have a night-time routine that once started I cannot stop. It takes me thirty minutes to brush my teeth."

"Thirty minutes!" I exclaimed.

"Indeed. My teeth are over one hundred years old and need to be kept in their prime. Otherwise I won't be able to feed properly, will I?"

"I suppose not." I was too tired for this shit.

"It was very selfish of your sister to disturb you like that," he said, sitting on the edge of my bed.

I was too tired to even protest, so as he carried on talking, I just closed my eyes again.

"Aaaarrrrrrgghhh," I screamed, as I woke seeing a vampire laid right beside me, although on the top of the covers and dressed.

"Aaaarrrrrrrgghh," the vampire screamed given he'd been asleep himself. He flew to his feet, fangs descended and eyes red, ready to attack and drain any threat.

The door burst open and Dela took one look at the crazed looking vampire before screaming. "Aaaaarrrggh." She jumped on top of me, protecting me with her body and making me scream again because the woman was bony.

I shoved her off me and turned to see Lawrie was now green-eyed and bemused. He arched a brow. "Are you inviting me for a threesome perchance?"

"Get out," I yelled. He strolled out laughing and said he'd meet me in the living room.

Dela turned to me. "I'm moving out. Milly and Tilly said I can room with them."

My jaw dropped for a moment. "I thought you were staying by my side to keep me safe?"

"Yeah, well, unless The Book of the Dead changes you're okay until Christmas Eve. Instead,

I'm going to go out as much as possible so I can keep an ear out for any enemies you may have made."

"In other words, you're going to date and enjoy yourself."

"That's just a nice bonus. I'll be doing this for my sister."

"You're all heart. Now get ready for work."

She beamed at me. "Don't you remember? I covered for you yesterday. I'm off today, so I'm going to move my things to the twins' place and then have a relax and get ready for tonight. We're all going to the bistro if you fancy joining us?"

"I can't. I'm having dinner with Lawrie, Mya, and Death at the Letwine mansion. I've been summoned to meet the elder, who I think wishes to be convinced I'm really serious about Lawrie."

"So, you're fucked then?"

"More than likely. Though Mya texted that she'll keep an eye on my future via the Book of the Dead app and says she'll intervene if Edmond becomes riled to the point he wants to drain me, so that's good."

"Sounds... terrible. If you get away early and we're all still around then come over."

"Will do, and don't forget tomorrow is book club

so make sure the twins know to come. It's the Christmas read."

Dela made mock sleeping gestures. "Book club is soooo borrrinnng."

"I love it and it might be my last one, so please come."

"This making me do things because you're going to die is going to get boring really quickly."

I smirked.

Indeed, it seemed I'd gone into a kind of hysteria today. Otherwise known as denial. I was following some of the steps of bereavement, only the person I was grieving was myself. Yesterday had been disbelief. I didn't know the order the emotions were supposed to come in, but denial was definitely hitting.

Of course, I wasn't going to die. I was clearly having a breakdown because I'd agreed to pretend to date the man I detested the most in the whole world.

Once I'd got myself washed and dressed for the day ahead, I met Lawrie in the living room and he agreed to come help out at the cupcake café given Dela was moving out. He was so ecstatic that she was moving that he offered to whizz her things over to the twins' house. After getting permission from them both over the phone to enter their home, he promptly moved all her furnishings within minutes. I didn't have the heart to tell him it could have all gone via the portals that we all had in our houses and business premises in the fell that he'd clearly forgotten about.

With a firm wide-eyed 'good luck' message communicated to me, Dela waved and left the store, leaving me alone with my new member of staff.

"Okay, let me show you the ropes."

"No need. I've watched you do it many, many times."

I started drumming my fingertips on the counter. "Watching isn't the same as doing, Lawrence."

"What would you like? Name a combination," he challenged.

"Okay." Oh I was going to have fun with this. "I'll have a half-soy, non-fat, decaf organic americano, with brown sugar, a touch of vanilla syrup, topped with whipped cream and chocolate and cinnamon sprinkles."

Disappointment crushed Lawrie's features. His shoulders slumped and his lips pouted. I almost felt sorry for him until he then smirked with those devilish green eyes twinkling. "Now of course when a customer is here, I'll perform at the ridiculous slow speed you non-vamps do everything at, but for now..."

I just saw a blur and then my exact order was placed in front of me, on top of a napkin. He'd also made a row of swans out of more napkins, and bunting from even more with heart shapes cut out in them all.

"God, I hate you."

"And don't I come here just to see that look on your face. It's why you must not die. I would miss not having you to torment. You've become like a pet of sorts for me to play with."

Folding my arms across my chest, I narrowed my eyes at him. "Clear this crap up. The customers will be coming in soon."

"Indeed they will." The smirk was back. "I can't wait to announce to everyone that we are in love."

I banged my head onto the countertop.

CHAPTER NINE

Lawrie

I hadn't been so excited about a day in a long time. I'd put the evening out of my mind because hell only knew how dinner with Edmond was going to pan out, but today... today could be a *lot* of fun. At my fake girlfriend's expense of course.

Callie opened the café's door, and the first customers of the day began to enter, smiling at her and saying, 'good morning'. It was interesting to watch people going about their daily business. As a vampire, I was used to stalking humans, and often I took my sweet time because there was no rush in my world.

Callie had told me to sit at the back of the café out of the way, and to act like a customer. My being there before the doors opened wouldn't surprise the regular residents of Gnarly who'd just presume I'd whizzed in front of them, given I was sitting with no drink. The newbies would be too distracted by the smells of the divine cupcakes to care. Anyhow, soon, I would reveal why I was there. My body tensed with glee at the thought, and I had an inner giggle.

But for now I let Callie get on with serving her customers, while I studied them all. Having to actually graft for a day did not appeal and so I was fine to play things this way unless the shop got too busy. Then Callie had told me I would have to step up.

Her customers were dull. Some just calling for takeout to take back to their own shops. It was interesting when Hettie from the chip shop came in. Her glare as she took a seat in the corner near the loos was palpable. Clearly new people had sat in her usual spot. I'd make sure I sat there tomorrow to annoy her further. It would serve her right for the measly portion of chips she gave me the last time I popped in. I might not need to eat but I still liked to enjoy the taste and she'd ripped me off. Just because her husband suffered with anaemia, she hated vampires with a passion. As if any of us would go near Trevor with his psoriasis. Ugh. I shuddered. One day I might corner Hettie just for the fun of it. See if she was all bark and no *bite*. Hahahahaha.

Yes, I was thoroughly enjoying myself until Stan's son walked in. Stan junior was built like a rugby player, buff, and tattooed. His hair was close shaved to his head which I knew some women dug. Not like mine which was a bit flowy, and he had scruff around his chin. Yes, some women loved that look, but not only that, he had charm aplenty given that his DNA came from the man who made dreams come true at Christmastime. Just one look at Stan jnr and you knew he made dreams come true every night of the goddamn year, and right now he was smiling at Callie. A great, toothy smile, complete with twinkling eyes, and oh look, he'd just reached up to grab a lemon cupcake from the top counter meaning his t-shirt rode up a little to reveal some toned abdomen. He was flirting with my fake-girlfriend, I just knew it. If I breathed I would have expelled air out of my nose. As Callie grinned back at him asking how she could help him, I decided now was as good a time as any to spread the word in Gnarly.

So, like any boyfriend would seeing a threat, I got out of my seat, moved swiftly behind the front counter, grabbed my fake girlfriend and pushed her up against the back wall, where I put my mouth on hers and claimed it as my own.

And she couldn't do anything about it, because to do would have given the game away. She actually had to kiss me back. From the tension in her body, she clearly wanted to stake me rather than kiss me, and that made it all the more glorious.

Breaking off the kiss, I turned around to Stan jnr, whose jaw had dropped slightly. It was a good look on the bastard as his jaw was so sculptured. "I must apologise, my friend, for the interruption. I was just filled with an irresistible desire to plant a huge kiss on my girlfriend's mouth. Right..." I smiled and shrugged my shoulders, fixing my gaze on Callie with what I could feel was a wicked glint in my eye. "I suppose I'd better make myself useful and clear a few tables, darling."

The cupcake café had gone silent. The usual cadence of chatter now completely gone. Some of the people in there this morning were regular customers and residents of Gnarly, and most would be aware of the derision Callie had felt for me up until this precise moment, so this... this was the best kind of gossip, and they'd not had any good gossip since Mya had arrived and the curse had been lifted.

Callie was looking shellshocked. Her fuchsia-pink lipstick was slightly smudged, her cheeks a great matching hue. She grabbed a napkin, and looking in a mirror at the back, she wiped her mouth, clearly giving herself a second before she turned back around.

"I must apologise, Stan jnr, for my boyfriend's inappropriate behaviour in the working environment."

"Not a problem, and oh, also, I've changed my name."

"You have?" I heard her ask him. I had to admit I was a little annoyed about the fact he'd not quizzed her on her new relationship, but instead had directed the attention back to himself.

"Yes, I can't be doing with all this Stan jnr stuff anymore. Now me and dad can date without the curse, a woman ringing for 'Stan' is just too confusing. I turned up for a date last night and the bird was fifty-six. She didn't mind one bit, but I had to make an escape in the end because it was a pottery making class and she wanted to re-enact the scene from Ghost with me."

"I totally get it. Dating can really *suck* sometimes."

I glared at her for that response from the table I was clearing, but Callie didn't look back at me. No, she was still all enraptured in conversation with whateverhisnamenowwas.

"So from now on it's Nick."

"Nick. Nice new name."

Huh, *Nick*. Had he changed his name as he was now a girlfriend stealer and that was more appropriate?

"It's my middle name. I'm Stanley Nicholas Anderson."

"So, if I abbreviate your first names, you're St Nick?" Callie laughed. It lit up her whole face and I clanged some mugs around, earning me a filthy stare. Did she not realise that negative attention was still attention? I blew her a kiss and watched her cheeks heat up again.

"Yeah." Nick returned a laugh as I walked behind the counter with the plates and cups.

"If you could scrape the plates into the bin out the back, empty the drinks down the sink, and empty and then load up the dishwasher, darling." Callie smiled sweetly at me. "By then I'm guessing we'll be ready for another round of clearing the tables and wiping them down. Oh, you haven't wiped them down yet, have you?" She pointed under the sink. "The cleaning stuff is under there, and oh, shoot, I forgot, just a moment." She disappeared out the back and returned holding a hairnet. "While ever you're working here you must wear an apron and this." She paused for a second, her eyes flashing with mirth, a crease appearing at the corner of her mouth as it aligned itself ready to laugh at my expense. Then she passed me the pink hair net.

I stood staring at it in my hand. A pink plastic hairnet, that I had to wear while Nick stood there looking like he was grabbing a snack before going on stage with The Chippendales, or just prior to chopping logs.

"Well, put it on and please hurry with the tables. If I get a rush of customers there'll be nowhere clean for them to sit."

She turned back to Nick. "They say not to mix business and pleasure don't they? I can see why. Now, you tell me what you want and it's on the house, both for the interruption, the delay, and to celebrate your new moniker."

I stood to my full height and placed the hairnet on my head. "Anything for you, snufflepuff," I sing-songed and then I walked out through the back to the bins.

The bitch knew full well what she'd asked me to do because as I lifted the lid off the bin, the most putrid smell of decaying food hit my above average sense of smell. I would not be defeated though. I scraped off the plates super-fast, and then returned, placing them in the dishwasher.

"Honey, though I usually know how to *turn things on*, I'm not sure with this machine, so could you come show me how?"

The twins had come in and giggled in unison from their place at the counter. Callie fake smiled and wandered over. "Sure."

As she approached, she muttered under her breath, "Stop it."

"You're the one who told me to load the dishwasher, now you want me to stop it?"

"You know what I mean. Milly and Tilly are now here asking me loads of questions after Dela has been updating them on you being my new 'boyfriend'. Also, none of my customers now seem to be in any rush to leave which means I'll earn less while they stretch out drinking their coffee, as customers won't queue for a table; not to mention the fact that having to pretend you're my boyfriend is only that one tiny incremental step away from being better than death."

"You're going to have to face facts, which is that not only do you have to act like my girlfriend now, you've got to completely have this as believable even to yourself by dinner tonight with Edmond, because if we don't fool him, I can't be your bodyguard anymore."

I watched as her eyes flicked towards where *Nick* sat with his lemon cupcake. "Fine. Go see if Nick can save your life instead, if you prefer him." Annoyingly, I could see her think about it for a second.

"Spider," I shouted, and I watched as Nick screeched and jumped up onto his seat. It was fifty-fifty whether it could have backfired on me or not if the twins had leapt at me in fright, but no, the rest of the shop's patrons were perfectly fine.

"Where, where?" Nick looked around.

"I'll leave you to it," I said, taking a step away from the counter. Callie's hand shot out.

"Stop. I'm sorry, okay? I know this situation is to help us both. Can we just call a truce? I'll forget what happened on our date and remember that you're here to help."

I hunched my shoulders and pulled at my earlobe. "I don't know. I'm not sure people here are going to believe we're together now seeing as I kissed you and in response you sent me out the back and then flirted with Stan jnr."

"Oh for God's sake." She exhaled loudly, and

then she grabbed me and pushed me up against the dishwasher, putting her arms around my neck and her lips on mine. She kissed me, totally instigated by herself in front of the whole café. I heard whoops and cheers and a simultaneous, "Go, Callie, go," from the twins.

But whereas I should have felt a deep satisfaction that I'd got her to do my bidding, instead, there was a slight unease. Because it hadn't been that long ago that I'd really liked this woman, and now she was kissing me and that kiss was good. So good that I didn't want it to stop.

I broke it off, pushing her away slightly, and I joked, "and you said we should be professional."

She beamed at me, and while I knew it was fake, others wouldn't. "I get it now. It's just *so hard* to resist. But you're right, we must try to focus on our work." She turned to the shop. "Sorry everyone, for the weird start to the day. As you can see, Lawrie and I finally sorted out our differences, and well, we're in love." She held up her hands in surrender. "Anyway, we moved in together last night and that's it for now. All our news. Now, excuse me, because we really must get some work done. I have a business to run!"

For the rest of the day, we were rushed off our feet and at one point Callie told me that she wished I could actually whizz around the place to clear up. We kept our public displays of affection limited to smiles at each other and being in close proximity at times, but other than that we kept it professional. With nothing much to see, customers stopped outstaying their welcome and in any case, if Callie pointed out someone doing so, I went over and hung around until they felt uncomfortable and either ordered something else or left. Being in the café wasn't so bad. Callie and I got in a routine, and I liked listening in on all the conversations around the place.

Finally, the last customer left, and Callie switched the sign to closed, walked over to a table and slumped over with a groan.

"It's been a great day for the business, but I am exhausted. I wish we weren't going out tonight because I could just fall into my bed."

"So do it," I shrugged. "Tell me what needs doing here to close up. I'll close the blinds, whip around at vamp speed, and you can have a nap before we go out." I looked at my watch. It was ten past six. "You can probably get an hour, and if you don't manage to sleep, at least you can rest a while."

Callie stretched. "I'm not going to refuse. While

you're around I've decided I'm going to make the most of it, instead of get annoyed by it."

"Erm, thanks. I think."

Callie relayed the list of jobs that needed doing and then left me to it. Within ten minutes everything was done and so I headed upstairs. If Callie was still awake, I'd let her know I was popping back to the mansion to get changed and would be back for her at five to eight. But she was fast asleep. She'd not even made it to bed. Instead, she was curled up on the sofa. I picked up the throw from the arm at the side of the sofa and I threw it across her. While she wasn't aware, I appraised her features. Her little button nose, her rosebud lips. The scattering of freckles across her cheekbones. Callie was extremely attractive. I sniffed the air because she smelled so good. Her general fragrance and her blood danced their aroma into my nostrils, and I felt my hunger for her grow. It wasn't the only thing that grew. (I meant my fangs, you filthy thinking individual.) And then she snored. A loud snort, that because of the colour of her hair and clothes made me think of a pig. It worked to break the spell and I left her there snorting like she was snuffling for truffles while I went quickly back to the mansion and got changed.

I returned at twenty to the hour because I'd

realised Callie would want time to get ready and I only hoped fifteen minutes was long enough as Edmond detested bad timekeeping. I needn't have worried because I returned to find Mya with Callie. They were in her bedroom.

For a moment I was frozen because Callie stood there in a black, figure-hugging satin wrap dress and high heels. She'd put some kind of fake hairpiece in so that her pink hair was scraped back and went into a black high ponytail. She looked amazing. We were on a date, so I decided to be truthful.

"You look incredible, Callie."

"Thanks, but you don't have to worry about us trying to convince Edmond. Mya has sorted it."

"She has?" I was so intrigued I let her dismissal of my compliment go.

Mya looked at me. "My power of suggestion. It's stronger than Edmond's because I'm not only vampire, I'm also part of Death's reign. The darkness of death cloaks me."

"How did you discover that?" I asked, bewildered.

"Jenny."

"Ah, the ex-librarian and curse-maker."

"Yes, she's now wanting to make amends and while she was in the libraries she read up on as much as she could. The Queen of the Wayward's thoughts could be cloaked, and she worked out that as I was also a vampire..."

"You could help cloak others, even against the strongest of vampires."

"Correct. Now of course we've not attempted it in front of our subject, but..."

"We can only try it," I said. "So you'll block Callie's thoughts?"

"Well, I thought that, but then Edmond would get suspicious at all the thought blocking, so instead, I think we need to go another route for tonight."

"Oh?"

"Yeah, I think I need to suggest to you two that you are actually in love," she said. "Just for the night."

CHAPTER TEN

Callie

I felt my eyes widen, like so much I thought my eyeballs might pop out and roll along my bedroom floor.

"Erm, how much practice have you had at this 'power of suggestion' thing because well, what if it gets stuck, and you make me permanently in love with this arsehole?"

"You could only be that lucky," Lawrie fixed me with his most uppity, looking-down-his-nose-at-me stare.

"Not much practice at all, but you two are shit out of luck at having any other way of convincing Edmond," Mya replied. "You can always do it your way and take a chance that the main male vampire, an elder, will be fooled by the thoughts of a diluted vampire and a fae born in the human world."

"Did you hear that?" Lawrie turned to me, this time wearing a look of camaraderie. "She's talking about us like we're trailer trash. A *diluted* vampire?"

"You know what I'm saying, Daddy dearest. You are nowhere near as powerful as the elder you're trying to fool. So if you ask me, you've both no choice but to let me try."

"Do it." I sighed. "Because otherwise Edmond is going to stab me with an iron sword for my treachery. I'm never going to get him to naturally believe I'm in love with Lawrie. I can barely tolerate him at the best of times."

"Yeah, do me as well, because my loathing of your best friend grows by the second, dear daughter." Lawrie's nose turned up like he was smelling manure. "As if I would be in love with the human world born fae."

"As if I'd love a *diluted* vampire," I spat back.

Mya's head had been moving from one of us to the other. "I thought I was supposed to be the child here. Okay, Lawrie, you first, because if I can do suggestion on you as my parent, then we know we're good."

"Very well," he acquiesced. "How shall we do this?"

"Come sit on the sofa because you're too tall for me to look into your eyes otherwise."

Lawrie moved as directed and sat as still as a statue on the sofa. It was unnerving. Like, all the time I'd known he was a vampire, and yet, it was at this moment, while he was still as a statue that he seemed his most dangerous, and I faced the reality that my protector was a vampire. A stealthy killer.

Mya began to speak while staring into those unblinking orbs.

"As Queen of the Wayward and a Letwine vampire, I call upon my powers of suggestion—"

"You're not knighting me, you're hypnotising me, child. Get on with it. Edmond does not suffer poor timekeeping."

"Lawrence Dickhead Letwine, you will believe that you are hopelessly in love with Callie Francis until I suggest otherwise."

I laughed and Lawrie's head moved in my direction. "What has tickled you, my darling?"

"Yeah, you're funny." I rolled my eyes at his acting.

The next thing I knew I was up against the wall with a vampire stroking my cheek while gazing lovingly into my eyes. "You find me amusing? That pleases me no end, my sweet. I am completely at your service."

"Fuck me, it's worked," Mya's voice rang out from behind me. "I'd better do you too, Callie, before you vomit."

I puffed air over my lips. "Yes, you'd better because there's a distinct possibility that's going to happen."

Mya managed to extricate me from Lawrie, seat me on the sofa and then she stared into my eyes. "Hang on. Vampires can't enthral other supes, can they?"

"We can't do some, but that's mainly because they wear enchantments to protect themselves. But I'm supercharged, so I probably can anyway." Mya puffed out her chest and flicked her hair. Then she grabbed my chin and began to speak.

"Ow."

"Keep bloody still then, you awkward mare."

"It's not going to work," was the last thing I remembered saying before Lawrence Letwine became the love of my life.

I knew deep inside that this was false, that it was

the thrall, but on the outside, my mouth and actions were a whole other ballgame.

I felt like I drifted over to Lawrie and I fell into his arms. "My love," my mouth said.

Mya snorted. "Oh my god, tonight is going to be the best night ever! I'm off to fetch Death and we'll see you there."

She disappeared and left us alone. Lawrie sauntered up to me. "I know we need to set off, darling, but before we do, I must do this."

He bent his head down to mine and kissed me. The coolness of his lips on mine made goosebumps tease across my flesh. The thralled part of me was going 'yeeeaaasssss, morrreeeee' and my arms curled around his neck, my lips parting to allow his tongue entrance. He kissed me long and hard, and it was the best kiss I'd ever had in my life. Even the inner me was aware of that, though outer me was overruling anyway.

Eventually he broke away. "It's time. Though I hate for my lips to be parted from yours, we must not dilly-dally."

"Yes, Edmond doesn't like latecomers. I get it." That was me talking, so it would seem I did have some control over myself, just not when it came to my 'relationship'. "I'm ready when you are," I told him and as he whizzed us both to the Letwine mansion, I realised that my body felt completely ready for other things with Lawrence Letwine. Somewhere deep inside I heard my inner self scream.

Though I knew we were going to a mansion, I really didn't expect the grand size and grounds of the place where we ended up. Lawrence had us appear next to a large Oak tree and once I'd got over my usual dizziness—which seemed to be improving each trip—I looked over his shoulder until he moved to my side, and I took in all the impressive greenery and well-tended flower borders.

"Wow, it's enormous."

Lawrie looked down at his groin area and then meeting my gaze followed my pointing finger to the grounds.

"Ah, yes, the mansion and its surrounds are huge. Come, my love, let's go meet Edmond." He offered me the crook of his arm and I took it and we walked towards the entrance. A huge wooden door creaked open as we arrived, and George Clooney stood there. I blinked twice and found that although he looked very much like him, as far as I knew, George didn't have fangs.

"Good evening, Lawrence, and this must be the

lovely Callie," the man said, and I quickly realised after the slight squeeze to my arm from my beloved that this must be the main man himself.

"Let them get into the house before you start your interrogation, Gramps," Mya yelled from behind. I heard Lawrie gasp, but Edmond only chuckled.

"Yes, you're right. It's just I'm intrigued as to who has begun to tame my most errant member of the family."

We followed Edmond and Mya into a grand sitting room: all leather Chesterfield sofas and dark, mahogany furniture. There was a wolf's head on the wall.

"Gramps, this is really not PC," Mya told him.

"That is the head of my greatest enemy, the wolf shifter, Dieter Pareti. It hangs there both to remind me of the best day of my life, and also to remind others that at my heart I am a killer."

Well, that was a nice ice-breaker to the evening. *Hello, I kill people, can I get you a drink?*

"Can I get you any refreshments?" he asked, a slight smirk to his lip which made me think he'd been listening in to my thoughts.

"Do you have vodka?" I asked. Fuck, if I was staying sober for this dinner now.

And then something amazing happened, because Death walked into the room and Edmond flinched, and it showed me that even the fiercest of creatures had weaknesses. Edmond might be undead, but he still walked the earth. Death had the power to take that away from him. Suddenly I felt a whole lot better.

So much so that I walked over to Death and hugged him. The tall, dark, brooding male froze for a moment and then patted my back, before gently pushing me away.

"Good evening to you too, Calendula."

"Well done, babe. See, you managed a hug." Mya beamed at him.

Death smiled back. It was possibly the most frightening thing I'd ever seen. Obviously unused to it, his mouth hung awkwardly like he was demented. Jack Nicholson hammering a door down, and the Joker had nothing on this expression. So much so that Edmond, who had the bottle of vodka in his hand to pour me a drink, poured and drank one himself first.

Maybe dinner wouldn't be so bad after all.

With drinks poured and handed out to those who wanted them, a gong sounded out, reverberating through the walls.

"Ah, dinner is about to be served. Please follow me," Edmond ordered, and we walked out of the sitting room, down the hall, and into the next room, a large banqueting hall, with a large table that seated twelve.

"I thought you'd have needed a bigger table with everyone here," I said, realising my stupidity the moment the words left my mouth. Of course, they didn't usually eat dinner, just drank it. I held my hand up. "Forget I said that."

Edmond directed us to where he wanted us to sit. I found myself sitting directly opposite him. Mya was to his left and Death to her left. Lawrie sat to my right, facing Mya. Edmond let us eat our starter, a prawn cocktail, before his interrogation began.

"It's been a long time since I entertained, but I simply couldn't resist the opportunity of meeting you, Callie. So tell me, what is it about Lawrie that has you both suddenly together and madly in love after I know you've spent the last few years hating him?"

And that was when my brain as I knew it left the building.

Love flooded through me. My stomach fluttered and I felt my pulse race. I moved my chair closer to Lawrie's so that my right leg touched his left, and as it did a tingling sensation, like an electric jolt sizzled through me. We shared a silly grin and I could *feel* our connection.

"There's a fine line between love and hate," I explained, looking at Edmond. I had no fear now in talking to the man because my love for Lawrie was so strong it could not be denied. "And yes, for a long time, hate was the side of the fence I chose to sit on after our disastrous date where his ex-meals turned up."

"I know of this. Go on."

"But I realised that the reason I hated him so much was through disappointment and jealousy. I'd looked forward to our date, and rather than feel special, I found myself cast aside while a slew of past-girlfriends, snacks, whatever you want to call them, turned up in front of me. And most of them were extremely beautiful. I do not have the highest self-esteem, and this made me feel less. Which is why after that, no matter what Lawrie did, I pushed him away. I decided to hate him because it was easier than facing my true feelings, that I liked him a lot."

My inner brain, currently squashed low down,

wriggled uncomfortably at these words that resonated with truth, but I was soon distracted when Edmond said,

"Ah, like, not love."

"That was then, Edmond, and forgive me, but with all due respect I don't like your tone, and your insinuation that our love is not the most incredible thing I have ever experienced. This man completes me." My hand grabbed Lawrie's and I squeezed it as we both grinned at each other. The love sensation burst through me again, like a fizzing excitement churning through like shook up champers.

"Something clicked between us the past couple of days. I realised that life is short, and you have to grab all opportunities that avail themselves to you. I decided to face my true feelings, that I love Lawrie with all of my heart, and I want to spend the rest of my life with him. And if you don't believe that, Edmond, well, that's up to you. I just ask that you be mindful of the fact that I have been nothing but respectful of you as the parental figure in my beloved's life and ask you might afford me the same honour as the girlfriend in Lawrie's life."

The room was silent, and Edmond's eyes flashed with red for a split-second. So quick, I felt I could almost have imagined it, were it not for the fact my stomach lurched with fear. I wondered if I'd gone too far.

"My apologies, Callie. You are right. I admit my experience with Lawrence is that he usually plays games, and I did feel that this was possibly another of them. But I can see you clearly do love him. I'm guessing you feel the same, Lawrence?"

All eyes moved to see what the vampire at my side would say to his elder.

"I do and I'd like your permission to propose, sir," Lawrie asked.

Inner me's buried thoughts went *what the actual fuck?*

CHAPTER ELEVEN

Lawrie

I was in love. There was a tiny little voice in my head trying to warn me of something, akin to a small butt itch that needed to be ignored while in company. I ignored it anyway because I'd never been so sure of a fact in all my life. Callie completed me. She was my lobster. I suddenly got what my sister had told me she was looking for after watching the complete series of *Friends*. In my sister's case a rich lobster.

I'd admired Callie for years, pursued her until our date that went wrong, and then treated her mean to keep her keen (okay, truth, I was being a sore loser). But now I realised with her eloquent speech that if she didn't care for me too, she wouldn't have been so hurt when my past loves walked in.

And now we were head over heels in love with each other. All was right with the world, and the next thing, the right thing, was to put a ring on the girl's finger.

Which I quickly realised I didn't have.

"Oh." I looked around, finding nothing that could do as an interim measure. This wouldn't do. I needed to propose, and I needed to propose tonight, like as soon as possible, this was the moment. The other dinner guests were looking at me strangely. "Excuse me a moment, all. Back shortly," I muttered and then I whizzed out of the room and appeared at the doorway of an esteemed London jewellers in the Westfield Centre. Thank goodness for late-night shopping.

I could get in the centre as I'd been here before and tricked someone into saying 'after you'. Now I hovered in the doorway, the inside brightly lit, the lights shining on the jewels to show off their glory.

"Can I help you?" An assistant had come out from behind the counter and walked outside, standing beside me as I looked in the window at the most expensive rings.

"Yes. I need a diamond so I can propose. Can you get me your most popular and I have no idea what size her finger is so I'll need to bring it back in about ten minutes."

A frown line appeared on her brow. "Why don't you come inside and I'll show you a selection of rings. You don't want to rush such an important decision. A proposal needs to be something your fiancée-to-be will remember forever. A tale to tell her family and friends."

I didn't have time for this shit. I stared into her eyes. "Give me the diamond ring that's most popular in the most average size immediately. I shall return it forthwith."

The assistant's eyes glazed over and robotically she went back inside the shop, opened a cabinet with a key, took out a ring and walked back outside to pass it to me.

"And please put it in a ring box." I sighed. I'd left my beloved waiting. Why hadn't I been better prepared with this proposal? Also, I realised I'd asked my male relative for permission to marry. I should have been asking Callie's father. Did she even have a father? I needed to find out more about her. But then, I would be spending the rest of my life, my very long life with her, and she aged slowly too, so what was the rush? Other than for this goddamn ring. Thank goodness the assistant was in the store on her own right now. At least I didn't have to enthral the whole shop.

"Here you go," the assistant said, reappearing. She handed me the ring and then stood there, awaiting my next instruction.

I'd whizzed back to the dining room before she could have expected a thank you.

I addressed everyone in the room as I appeared back in front of them. "My hearty apologies for that interruption, and also Edmond, while I would like your blessing on our potential union, I do intend to propose anyway regardless of your decision," I announced.

I thought Edmond might bite my head off (with words, though I'm sure he'd have actually bitten someone's head off at one point, he was a very evil, killer vampire elder), but he remained silent. Instead, it was Mya who spoke. "You sure about that, Dad? You've only just reconciled. Why not leave it until, say, the new year?"

My lip curled and I wrinkled my nose. "Absolutely not. I don't want to spend another moment of my life without having this woman in a verbal contract to be my wife."

"Wow. That's so romantic." Mya rolled her eyes.

Edmond cleared his throat. "I give you my

permission, Lawrence Letwine, to propose. I never actually thought I'd see the day. This is quite something, and very different to what I'd expected to happen this evening."

"Me too," Mya said.

I turned to Callie who had been silent since my return. Her face had kind of seemed frozen. Maybe the starter hadn't agreed with her stomach? Prawns could be dodgy. I turned her chair around to face me and then I dropped to one knee.

I noticed Mya was videoing the whole thing on her phone. That was good. My future wife and I would have the moment recorded forever.

"Calendula Francis. My heart no longer beats, but when I'm with you I imagine it does. No other woman, and I have enjoyed the carnal knowledge of many as you know, has come close to how I feel about you, and we haven't even slept together yet. You are the yin to my yang, the moon to my star, the jelly to my ice-cream, the night to my day, the tomato sauce to my fish fingers. You both complement me, and also push me to be a better man. I love you, and I want to spend the rest of my life with you. So, Callie, will you marry me?" I opened the ring box.

"Yes," she announced with a squeal, holding out her hand. "Oh my god, oh my god, oh my god." I went to slide the ring on, but it was too large. Bless her, her hand was shaking. I think it was nerves, but it almost looked like she was trying to pull it away from me. A very weird nervous jerk.

"We will deal with the ring being too large in a moment, my beautiful new fiancée," I told her happily.

Pulling her to her feet, I tipped her back and kissed her like I'd seen in movies. Then I turned to the others. Edmond was smiling; Death was his usual brooding self, sat with his arms folded across his chest looking bored; and Mya widened her eyes at me and shrugged her shoulders. Whatever. I wasn't on cloud nine, I was on cloud nine billion. "I give you my fiancée." I said to the others, holding up Callie's ring bearing hand, before I stared at her and beamed. I couldn't believe she was mine. "Now if you could just bear with us for another moment." Grabbing hold of Callie's hand, I whizzed us back to the shop.

The assistant startled as we appeared in front of her. Callie lurched and placed her hand on the counter. "Whoa. When am I going to get used to that?" She stared at the assistant and grinned like the Cheshire cat. "I'm engaged." She held out her hand, the diamond spinning to the back with the ring being so loose.

"I've brought the ring back as you can see," I told the assistant, whose name badge said she was called Bea. I was sure I heard her mumble, 'oh thank God,' under her breath. "My fiancée may now choose her own ring. Callie, pick whatever you like, darling. I'm loaded, but don't take too long because we have guests waiting, remember?"

She fiddled with the one on her ring finger so the diamond was back where it should be. "I love this one. It's the one you proposed with, so, Bea, do you have this in my size?" Callie asked.

"Let's get you measured and find out," she replied. I saw her take a deep breath as she drew the key out of her pocket and placed the old ring that Callie had now slipped off her finger back in the display case.

All in all, I felt pretty good about myself as I left the store. I might have enthralled the assistant at the start of the evening, but as the store was coming to a close she'd earned a *very* good commission that meant now we were *all* smiling.

Callie couldn't stop looking at the Princess-cut diamond on her ring finger.

"Are you ready to go back to dinner?" I asked.

She pressed her lips together. "Hmmm. I suppose so. Though it would be nice to not have to share the evening with the others. I wish it was just us two, somewhere moonlit, where we could stare at the stars romantically and celebrate our amazing love for each other."

I clapped my hands together. "Then let's do that. You're right. This is *our* evening. Edmond wanted us to come to dinner and we went, right? They'll all understand if we don't return, and we'll throw an engagement celebration as soon as possible, so we can all get together again. Now I know just the place we can go, and I also know that right now the owners aren't in."

I whizzed her to the top of the hill just outside of Gnarly Fell, where Mya and Death's home sat amongst the gnarled trees the place was named for. We sat on a carved oak seat overlooking Gnarly and gazed down at the village and up at the moon and stars. It was a clear night and the stars twinkled like they wished to complement the diamond on my fiancée's finger.

I had a *fiancée*. I was going to be *married*. I was so flipping *excited*!

I held Callie's hand, bringing it up under the

moonlight. The diamond sparkled. "Callie Letwine to be."

"Not Parsons then, your real surname?"

"No, my sweet. That died when I did. Anyway, did you know my initials spelled lamp? Lawrence Alexander Marcus Parsons. L.A.M.P. Lamp."

Callie giggled. "That's made me realise I'm definitely not becoming Parsons."

"Why?"

"My name is Calendula Rose Aster Francis. My initials after marrying you would spell crap."

I laughed alongside her. "Calendula Rose Aster Letwine it is."

Callie sighed happily. "This is crazy. We only just got back together, but it feels so right and even though we don't know each other that well, if I have only a little time left on earth, why not get engaged quickly, right?" She made a tiny 'ugh' sound.

"What was that?"

"I don't know. It must be some reaction to tonight's events. All I know is after that noise I have just felt love for you absolutely overwhelm me. I have butterflies, Lawrie, when I look at you. I never thought I'd meet my one before my potential demise. I do hope you can save me."

"You need to make that bucket list, darling. If I

can't save you, I will make every one of your dying wishes come true. That's how much I adore you."

"Oh, Lawrie."

We kissed again, long and slow, and then she said the words my ears had long wanted to hear.

"Let's go back to my place."

I embraced her and took us back into her living room. Callie left the room, and I presumed was going to the bathroom to 'freshen up'.

I actually felt nervous. Me! Lawrence Letwine, lover of many. Giver of an incredible number of climaxes. But this time I was in love. I didn't want to just bone my new fiancée, I wanted to make love to her. That's if I'd got her meaning of 'let's go back to my place' correct, and she didn't just mean she'd wanted to go home.

"Lawrie," Callie called out and I followed her voice into her bedroom. Where she stood stark naked.

"You're wearing far too many clothes, my fiancé," she said, arching a brow and beckoning me towards her with a frosted pink fingernail.

It seemed my dreams were about to become a reality.

The beauty about being a vampire with super-speed meant when I needed things to be quick, for example, in removing all my clothes, I was an expert. However, when it came to enjoying the body of my new fiancée, I was taking that one slow. I stalked towards my prey, knowing I'd already caught her, but now intended to make her mine. My eyes roamed her body taking in her pale skin, and her perfect bosoms with their rosy-pink nipples. My cock was harder than the removal of Excalibur by anyone but King Arthur, and I watched as Callie's eyes dropped to it. She licked her lips with anticipation.

Placing my hand behind her neck, I pulled her towards me and kissed her lips. I craved the feel of her mouth on mine. Her body fit alongside my own, those breasts pushed up against me. Her skin prickled with goosebumps; I guessed both with the coldness of my body meeting her warmth, as well as the sensations and her arousal. And she was aroused alright. I could *smell* it. Like honey and sunshine.

My hands moved to fist in her hair as she moaned into my mouth. It was no good, I needed to taste her. Needed to have that sweet blood sing in my mouth. Just a touch. For us to mate via the vampire kiss before we mated as fated mates. For that's what I felt we were, meant to be together. It was our destiny.

My mouth left hers and trailed down her neck. She shivered under my touch.

"May I take a nip? Begin to make you properly mine?" I asked with reverence.

"Yes," she acquiesced, her words a plea from her lips, uttered on a mix of a moan and a gasp.

I licked at the skin where her neck curved into her shoulder, anaesthetising it with my vampire saliva, and then I bit down.

"Ooooooh," Callie moaned in ecstasy as her blood mixed with my bite.

"Fuucccccck," I said as her sweet taste hit my tongue.

"What the hell have I fucking done?" screamed my daughter from behind us.

CHAPTER TWELVE

Callie

I looked over my shoulder dreamily and thought I could see Mya standing in the room. Weird. I was enraptured. My head whirled like I was drunk on love, and the sensations flipping through my body and heading south? I had no words to describe them, but I knew I needed Lawrie's cock there because once that hit the spot, I was going to hit my O.

"Ugh." There was that weird sound coming from me again. What was going on?

I found myself moved to one side where again, I kind of saw Mya. She seemed to shimmer in my vision like a reflection in water. I vaguely heard her speak. It was like my ears were full of water. Was I drowning?

"I release you from the thrall of love."

Mya didn't become any clearer visually, although I could now hear her much better. I still felt quite drunk. Had I been drinking? Looking down, I realised I didn't seem to have any clothes on.

"Huh?"

"Excuse me a moment," Mya said and then she leaned in and licked my neck!

"*Whoa.* What are you doing, you freak?" I yelled as things started becoming a slight bit clearer. Lawrie was in my room, and *did he not have clothes on as well? What the hell?* "Have you given me that date drug and you're trying to get me involved in some kind of sick three-way, because I'm not up for that." I slumped onto my bed.

Mya moved to my bedroom door, returning with my robe and she helped me wrap it around myself. "I was just sealing your bite," she said.

That was too much for my brain to process, so I buried the word 'bite' down until later and asked the question bothering me the most right now. "Why was I naked? Why is he naked and just standing there?"

"I have tasted you and I have been frozen in the moment, my sweet," Lawrie said, coming to kneel at my feet. He still wasn't clear in my vision. Whatever I'd drunk or taken needed to wear off quickly. It was annoying me now. I needed coffee! I went to get up, but Mya pulled me back down.

"I am not having sex with you, Mya. Stop it." I pushed her away from me, but she didn't actually move. "God, stupid bloody vamp strength. You'd better not take advantage of me, because I know people who will pull your fangs and the rest of your teeth out and sell them on the black market, and they'll cut me in and I'll buy some jewellery to remember my retribution." I waved a hand in warning at her and then saw it had a ring on it. I was clearly verrrry drunk or asleep and dreaming. "I'm gonna lie down," I said. "Remember, if I wake up and my robe's been moved, Tooth Fairy's coming for you." I shook my fist at Mya and then laid down.

My eyes opened to the brightest winter sunshine coming through a crack in the bedroom curtains. As memories began to assail my mind, I sat up, plumping my pillows, and knocked the alarm button off.

"That was the weirdest dream," I said to myself, rubbing my eyes and trying to stop squinting. I was on my own in my room, dressed in my pyjamas, not the robe of my dreams, but, God, the dream had been so vivid. I'd dreamt that I was going to die, Lawrie Letwine was going to save me, we'd got engaged, and I'd let him bite me before Mya had come and interrupted us. I laughed heartily. What a vivid imagination.

Getting out of bed, I walked over to the curtains, pulling them wide open. And as I did so the diamond on my ring finger caught the sunshine.

I screamed like I was being murdered by a serial killer and within seconds there were two people in my room. Mya, and Lawrence Letwine—who was wearing my pink robe.

Memories assaulted my brain like hail smashing down onto the top of a caravan.

"What did you do to me?" I yelled at Mya. "It was like I was in a coma, and I could hear everything, but I couldn't make anyone understand, even myself. I couldn't stop being in love with... with..." I just pointed at Lawrie.

"Well, that's charming, and after I dropped five grand on a diamond engagement ring for you too." He huffed. "You weren't the only one *under the influence.*" He narrowed his eyes at Mya. "And I don't mean alcohol." Lawrie turned back to me. "You tried to fight it. I heard and saw it. You kept going 'ugh' like you had food stuck in your throat and at one point you did this weird jerk with your hand while I was trying to put a ring on it." A look of amusement passed his features.

"If you do a Beyoncé dance, I am going to stake you. The only weird jerk around here is you." I went to remove the engagement ring from my hand, but trouble was, it was really beautiful, and I didn't want to give it back. How could I keep an engagement ring but not be engaged to Lawrie?

"We're engaged now whether you like it or not, so you might want to keep the ring on." Lawrie sighed. "My vampire family will all know now. Today we need to tell your family and friends before it leaks over from the mansion, or from Mya. She's not exactly known for her restraint."

"Fine." I acted like it was an ordeal, when secretly I was ecstatic to wear a pretty diamond and it meant I had got engaged in my lifetime, even if it was to Lawrie. I felt so strange because I was aware of what I'd said and done and my inner resistance, but then when Mya had arrived, I'd just felt dreamy and...

"You bit me!"

"You let me."

"I can't believe you bit me." My voice was getting louder by the minute.

"Hang on, girlfriend. I asked very nicely and I was brainwashed at the time. Now whether we were enthralled or not, I won't have you diss my bite. A vampire's bite is very, very important, and you enjoyed it very much."

I thought on his words and remembered the dreamy sensation again.

"Okay, fair enough. I'll let you have that one. It was quite nice. By the way, you have a really good physique, I'll give you that. I rather thought you'd be scrawny."

"Why thank you. I must say, you have fantastic boobs."

"Aww, thanks." I looked down my pyjama top where after a quick glance I decided I agreed with him. I did have a great rack.

"And I thought this situation couldn't get any weirder," Mya said.

"You are in so much trouble with me." I put my hands on my hips.

"Because of me you're engaged, not dead at the hands of Edmond. So if you feel pissed off take a look at that diamond, and thank the Lord that I got back when I did before you consummated everything, because having his bite on your neck and then having sex would make you his vampire mate. His consort. And only your death would be getting you out of that one. That's a betrothal you can't break, or the Letwine family would kill you themselves."

"That can't be right. You must have bitten one of your many lovers before you had sex with them before," I questioned Lawrie.

"Yes, but not on their *neck...*"

"Gross," I announced while my mind went there, wondering what it would be like. *For goodness' sake, Callie, you have the shop to open, and the book club tonight.* It was time to get ready and try to get my head together while I had a shower.

With no sign of my sister, who to be honest I didn't expect to turn up for work now she'd moved out unless I ordered her to, Lawrie agreed to open up the café and told me to go enjoy a long soak in the tub. I took him up on his offer as I felt I needed a decent amount of time to myself to think about the events of last night. As I slipped below the frothy bubbles, the heat soothing my tired body, I felt the muscles in the back of my neck start to unkink. I'd gone for a soothing, mild lavender bath soak, and I inhaled the slight fragrance as I leaned back and rested my head on my bath cushion. Step-by-step, I took myself through the events of the evening from the beginning, remembering how I'd acted at the proposal and when we'd sat at the top of the mountain, and ending with getting bitten and Mya's interruption.

I'd tried to fight from deep inside, to resist, but it had been to no avail. But I wasn't angry, and I should have been angry. I should have felt defiled. Instead, I could only remember the feel of Lawrie's lips on mine, and how I'd felt when he'd bitten me.

It's the venom. It's still in your system, babes. I reassured myself. I spent much of the time in between memories admiring the diamond on my finger. Lawrie was telling the truth; he'd clearly dropped quite a bit of money on this sparkler. The money didn't count though. It was just how exquisite it looked, clearly a stone of merit, and on a thick platinum band he'd told me before my bath. He was only getting this ring back if he had to prise it off my cold, dead body. If he managed to save my life, then I was keeping it after our 'fake split'.

All in all, I wasn't doing too badly out of this

bodyguard arrangement if you excluded the fact I might die. In all the time I'd got Dela to work in the café, she'd never once let me have a lie in, or a bath. It was always her who came in late and left early. I loved my sister dearly, but she could be quite selfish. It was because she didn't need the money. We had an allowance from being tooth fairies. I was the one who'd decided on a business so I could diversify from just sending sweet treats to supermarkets to destroy teeth, although I had got her agreement to work there first. What I'd not done was explain I wouldn't mind if she opened up occasionally. Still, knowing Lawrie was capable of holding down the fort while I enjoyed a bath made me feel excited. A girl could get used to that.

No, you couldn't. For goodness' sake. Remember who he is. The man who treats women like a packet of instant soup, quickly forgettable as you're soon hungry again.

As blissful as the bath had been, I couldn't leave Lawrie on his own much longer and I also needed to start some baking. Reluctantly, I got dried and dressed and made my way down to the café. The morning rush had subsided, and the place was half-full. Lawrie had everything under control as I knew he would, and all the customers seemed happy. The only person who didn't seem happy was Lawrie.

"I'm sorry. I took too long, didn't I? I won't take advantage like that again. It was just so nice."

"What?" He looked distracted.

"Oh, I thought you were annoyed with me because I was in the bath so long."

"Oh, no. You were fine. Hopefully you enjoyed it."

"It was just what I needed." I changed tack. "So is it that you've remembered what you had to endure last night?"

"No, Callie. To be honest I have no regrets, other than my bank account has a few fewer thousand in it, but I'm filthy rich, so hey ho. I got a few snogs with a beautiful woman, saw her naked, and tasted her. All in all, I'd call it a good night out myself."

I laughed. Happy he'd decided to see the situation with humour. But still, Lawrie looked uncomfortable. There was something he wasn't telling me.

"What did you do?"

"Huh?"

"You look constipated. So what did you do? Did you fuck orders up or something?"

"No. All was perfect."

"Then what is it?"

"Nothing."

"Lawrie, whatever it is I need you to tell me. Because not knowing will eat me up inside. My mind needs to be on my work and then tonight's upcoming book club. Not on what crawled up your arse and died."

"There's nothing up my arse. I have regular colonics to rid myself of anything that comes from digesting human food."

I closed my eyes and took a very deep, very long breath.

"Tell me now and I'll flash you my boobs again."

"As much as I would absolutely love that, I don't think this is in your best interests."

Covering us up by the counter and casting my eyes over the customers to ensure no one was looking, I moved closer to Lawrie and placed my hand over his groin. "That's not playing fair," he groaned. Then I squeezed, just enough that he got the threat.

"Tell me what the fuck is up with you, or I'll make sure this package is never available for delivery again," I warned.

"Fine. You'll wish you hadn't pushed me on this."

I let go as he stomped over to the microwave.

Pushing his fingers underneath he pulled out a piece of folded paper and handed it to me.

My fingers unfolded the paper and I smoothed it out on the counter as I took in the words.

Callie Francis
You better watch out.
I'm coming for you.

The note was typewritten on plain paper. "I n-need to take this to the police," I said.

"I already did. Before I opened the shop," Lawrie replied. "I came downstairs to open up and it had been posted through the letterbox. I whizzed straight to Dirk, a vampire I know who's a cop. We need people on the inside, see, for when vampires go rogue, or accidentally drain someone. Anyway, there's nothing on it, no evidence."

I felt my shoulders sink under the weight of his news.

"I swear, I won't let anything happen to you, Callie. I'll stay by your side until we change your fate."

Lawrie opened his arms and I went into them. When I had a real life enemy, I wasn't going to turn down a comforting hug from someone who, whatever their own intent, was helping me.

Right now, I had more to worry about than hating on Lawrence Letwine. I closed my eyes, sank my head into his chest, and as his hand stroked the back of my head, I whispered, "Thank you."

CHAPTER THIRTEEN

Mya

We'd waited thirty minutes for the lovebirds to return last night before we'd given up and decided to eat the evening meal. We might get no nutritional value from it, but we still enjoyed the taste. However, after finishing a gorgeous chicken dinner, I began to suspect that the errant duo weren't returning.

"It doesn't take this long to change an engagement ring, does it?" I asked Edmond and Death.

"I have no idea how you think I might know the answer to that question," my boyfriend answered. "How long before rigor mortis, yes? Engagement ring choosing? Wrong guy."

"How very romantic you are." I rolled my eyes heavenward.

"They can't help you," Death quipped. "Or those down below."

"Edmond, do you know how long it takes to choose an engagement ring?" I decided to direct my questions to someone who might have been engaged in his long years.

"Oh, it can take forever. However, my dear, you can follow his scent and whizz to wherever they went. I do feel Lawrie is not teaching you everything you need to know as a vampire. You must come to me once a week for lessons."

"That would be amazing, and of course, I forgot about the scent trail. Back soon."

That was when I'd followed my father's scent and found it led me to Callie's bedroom.

After I'd dealt with those two, I'd quickly gone back to appraise Edmond and Death of the situation and then returned to Callie's, where I'd stayed until she'd come round a little. The bite had made her blood drunk.

Now I stood in the kitchen drinking a bottle of O-neg while I felt the eyes of my boyfriend on me.

"You told her she's going to die, didn't you?"

"Ooh, I forgot to tell you, the twins are doing a buy one, get one free if you need to stock up on black cloaks."

"Mya..."

I slumped forwards, wiping my mouth on the back of my hand and then sighing when I remembered it wasn't like water and had left a large red streak. I went to wash my hands.

"I couldn't help it. I didn't give her the details. I just said she would die on Christmas Eve."

"And is that the reason for her sudden engagement to Lawrence? Is she trying to fit in as much as she can before her demise?"

Reluctantly, I filled him in on events to date.

"So the engagement is a lie, as is their relationship. Seems a waste of whatever days she has left to me."

"Are you sure you can't change it?"

"I'm sure. Only circumstances outside my control can do that. But, Mya, you are not supposed to speak of what you find. I'm surprised the book hasn't punished you for it."

I shuddered. The last time I'd angered The Book of the Dead it had knocked me unconscious.

"Well, what would you do in the same situation?"

"I've been in that situation, Mya. I know everyone's deaths. I tell no-one. Well, except now you know too. But you can't tell people. It can cause problems."

"Like what?"

"Well like Callie will now start doing things differently to what she would have before. It can have an effect on other people's lives. So maybe now, Callie's death will be prevented, but someone else will die."

"Oooh. Can I choose the swapsie? Because Ethel on Twisty Way has really bad breath from her three remaining rotting teeth. She's way past her sell-by date."

"Mya!"

Oh dear, he was getting annoyed now. You couldn't tell by looking at him because he always looked broody or moody anyway, but his tone of voice had changed.

"It was just a suggestion. I'm new here, so sometimes new people make suggestions on new ways to do things."

"And I'm the supervisor here and I'm here to teach you that death has its routine and you have to follow the exact process as it's always been, or you run the risk of changing things, and that's not good."

"Fine. I'll not tell anyone else about their death. Anyway, The Book of the Dead didn't tell me who kills her which is weird."

"The book decides what information it wants to release and when. It clearly feels you aren't ready to know. Probably because it doesn't trust you and thinks you'll tell her."

"It sucks."

Death hung around a little, chewing on his lip like he wanted to ask me something.

"Out with it."

"The talk of engagements last night. Is that something you might want in the future?"

I shook my head. "We've been dating for two minutes, so I don't think you need to panic about that anytime soon. Anyway, I like living in sin. It feels kinda dirty. So, no, I don't think I do want that in my future. White's never been my colour, and especially now my skin is even paler. But if I change my mind, I'll let you know. Okay?"

"Okay. Good. I didn't think you'd want to be my chattel... my ball and chain... Mrs Death."

I opened my mouth to launch a row of expletives at him, but he was gone, his exiting laughter ringing in my ears.

I thought about my friend. Had I done the right

thing in letting her know what the book said? Well, it was too late now. All I could do was keep an eye on the book (and I also had the app of it on my phone) and see what it told me. I pressed into the app. It was still exactly the same entry.

Unfortunately, at the moment, Callie was still fated to die.

CHAPTER FOURTEEN

Lawrie

A guy could get used to hearing all these compliments.

"Thank you so much."

"That was wonderful."

"So tasty."

"I feel satisfied, but still crave more."

Alas, rather than it be from anyone I ever took to bed, this time it was from customers tasting my fiancée's baking. She did serve the most delicious, sweet treats, it had to be said. The aroma of baking flittered through from the kitchen as Callie brought fresh cupcakes through to the front counter. And what was that? Oooh, she'd done her special red velvets. There were three of them in a box and she put them in front of me on the counter. The special red velvets had O-neg in the bun and the frosting. My mouth watered.

"That's my official thank you. For you helping out this morning. There are another nine in the back too."

As I wasn't currently serving, I opened the box and brought one up to my mouth. Yet, although it was mouth-wateringly delicious, and I visually and audibly showed my appreciation, there was something lacking. It took me a moment to realise what it was. I'd tasted Callie's blood last night, and this just didn't measure up.

"I know this is weird, but I feel something has changed between us since last night," Callie said. Her tongue flicked over her bottom lip. She was nervous. Oh goodness, she felt it too, didn't she? That we had a connection? That something was actually happening between us.

"I feel the same way," I replied. "There's been a definite shift since we got... close."

"That's it. I don't know if it's connected with the bite, but I feel closer to you."

I moved a little nearer to her. "Go on."

She took a visual deep breath. "Gosh, this is difficult for me to say, because I never imagined this would be the case between us..."

Placing my hands on both of her forearms I got ready to drag her into my embrace.

"... but somehow you've become a friend."

Friend.

Friend?

FRIEND?

Oh my god, I had just been friend-zoned. This had never happened to me before. I needed to sit down. I let go of her arms and moved to the counter.

"Are you okay?"

"Must be the O-neg. I'm feeling a bit weird." *Like I might fucking cry.*

What was happening to me? The amazing lover that was Lawrence Letwine. The cad. The rogue. The charming and debonair vampire.

Then it hit me. Like I'd been hit by lightning. It was like for a second the fork was on me and it fried my brains.

I was in love with Callie Francis. I'd had a taste and now I wanted her. All of her.

Was there anyone who did 'love exorcisms'? This could not be. Because she liked me as a friend. Oh no, I wasn't having unrequited love with this woman. I wasn't showing her any vulnerabilities. A woman had done that to me before, made me feel less of a man. It's why I'd ended up a vampire in the first place. No, I'd return to being the vampire I'd been before I became her protector. I'd protect myself.

Friend. Huh.

I realised Callie was hovering and asking me if I was okay.

"I'm fine, babes. Obviously just a little too much of the O-neg after the nip I already had last night, but I do really appreciate the gesture of you making them for me. I'll take the others back to the mansion and share them because they love your cupcakes as you know."

"Yes, that's probably for the best. Anyway, I'm glad you feel the same way, about us being friends."

"Oh, that's not what I'd been going to say, Callie."

"Oh?"

"I'd thought you were going to say now we'd seen each other naked, it seemed a shame to not keep doing it. I was going to offer to sleep with you every night in your bed now. There really doesn't need to be any barriers between us now I've seen everything."

There was a beat of stillness and silence.

"Jesus. I thought we'd finally got somewhere, but you're still a complete pig."

"Oink."

She stalked off, mumbling about doing more baking under her breath, and went through to the back kitchen.

My skin felt like it was itching. Like I'd put on a woollen jumper. But I knew it was because I'd gone back to being the man with the crush on a girl, and that crush was yet again unrequited. But then the bell above the door jangled as a customer came in and I buried those feelings once more and kept calm and carried on.

Callie was taking off her apron as I walked into the kitchen. "So I'm off to book club. Mya will be there, so you can go do whatever it is you want to do tonight. Drain a poor, unsuspecting female; cut someone down with your biting tongue; go rest in a coffin. You're free of me."

"Darling, I'll be accompanying you to book club." I leaned against the worktop.

"Why? Might I die of a paper cut?"

I shivered thinking of the last paper cut I'd had. It had healed quickly but it still had stung like a bitch.

"No, you might die at the hands of whoever

threatened you, and as yet, we don't know who that is. Maybe it's someone from book club who resents losing hours of their valuable life to the last tedious tome you chose for them."

"Ha ha," she replied and then stood thinking. "Do you think it could actually be someone from Gnarly? Someone I know?"

"We don't know, do we? And so that's why I will be going with you. Also, while we are there you will show off your engagement ring and let everyone know the happy news that we are now betrothed."

"Ugh."

"Oh I know, sweetie." I mock pouted. "It'll be so difficult showing that big diamond off to everyone."

At that Callie did actually smirk. "Okay, you got me there."

"Women."

"What do you mean, 'women'?" Callie was back to that 'hands on hips' stance she did so well.

"You look forward to book club, you go to have a chat with all your friends, but then you want to play 'look at my diamond' and get all competitive. You're not all really friends at all, are you? It's a place for you all to gossip. I bet you've annoyed one of them so much, they're trying to kill you. I know at times I've been tempted to strangle you with my bare hands."

"Huh. In the past your life has been at *stake*, matey."

"I'm not your mate."

"Dead right. No biting and consummating here."

I appraised her up and down and then followed it with a lusty wink. "You want to ask yourself if that would have been the case had Mya not come crashing into the room when she did."

"I was enthralled!"

"Yeah, by my penis."

A cupcake came flying in my direction, but I swiftly whizzed behind her and went, "Boo," in her ear, making her jump, as I stroked her neck where I'd bitten her the night before.

"Get your hands off me."

"Go get ready for book club," I ordered. "I think it'll be lots of fun."

I laughed as she stomped off out of the room.

The book club took place in a room in the community centre. It was a sparse room with magnolia-coloured painted walls. There were notice boards that advertised classes and also gave health and safety information, fire evacuation instructions etc, and there were also paintings that had clearly been created by participants of a beginner's art class because they certainly weren't Monet. I had to admit that I was a bit of an art snob due to being around the mansion where some original paintings hung.

Black plastic chairs were spaced out around a small, beech coffee table in the centre of the room and there was a longer, rectangular, beech table at the back that had black decanters on it with little taps. One said tea and one coffee. Beside the back table was a small fridge that I presumed held the milk and anything else the paranormals drank and ate that needed to be chilled.

Hanging back, I let all the women take their seats as I presumed some might claim the same one each time, and people could get funny about such things as I'd witnessed in Callie's café. I walked in and the heads of everyone there swivelled in my direction. Ignoring them, I pulled up a chair between Callie and an older lady.

"Oooh," the woman who was about seventy said. "Fresh totty."

"Behave yourself, Delores," another one said, but then she also stared at me and batted her eyelashes.

Mya called the group to order.

"So tonight, we will discuss any books you read

last week and then I'm going to suggest everyone reads a special Christmas book. But firstly, let's address the elephant in the room."

Delores interrupted. "That's not nice, sugar. He's not even fat. In fact, he needs some good ol' fashioned feeding up. Drop by mine anytime, sugar. I make a mean lamb cobbler."

"That's not what he eats, Delores." The other woman, Barb, said. "He's a vampire."

"Oh, you're one of them there folks who doesn't eat anything but plants?"

"That's a vegan. He eats you. Drains your blood," Barb helpfully added.

"Whhaaaat? Until I'm passed on? Still, what a way to go."

"ANYHOW," Mya recalled the two old ladies' attention. "Lawrie is here because he and Callie have some news. Over to you, Callie."

All eyes were on Callie now, and she flushed slightly. "Some of you may have heard the news from people who visit the café that Lawrie and I are now together. And well..."

"Yes, honey?" Delores asked. "Are you up the duff?"

I decided to sweep in. "I asked Callie to marry

me, and she said yes. The curse of Gnarly Fell is indeed lifted and everyone is free to love once more."

Dela chose that moment to walk in. "Say what? You're marrying Lawrence? That progressed quickly." I saw her mouth, "I thought you hated his guts." To which she received an eye communicated STFU from both me and Callie.

Fenella clapped her hands. "Oh this is absolutely wonderful news. Not only that you two are betrothed, but also that it shows the curse is truly lifted. We shall have a village celebration. Who's up for helping me to organise it?" All there eagerly accepted Fenella's invite; well, the ones who weren't clambering to get a good look at Callie's engagement ring. A few of the villagers her age were clearly envious, and Callie thoroughly enjoyed showing her bling off. For a moment she looked like any newly engaged woman, not one facing a lack of a wedding and her own demise.

Lawrie, you must somehow get this ridiculous sympathy and lovesickness out of your system, I scolded myself.

"Let me congratulate you, sugar," Delores said grasping tightly onto my thigh. She leaned over and ignoring my proffered cheek kissed me straight on the mouth. The shock made me open wide and then she stuck her tongue in.

"I can pass on happy now," she said and leaned back in her chair smiling away to herself. Meanwhile I wanted to leave and start my in-depth tooth brushing regime.

There was scant time given to the Christmas book choice as the talk became that of the celebrations due to take place this coming Saturday. Apparently, Gnarly didn't need long to put a party together. The mood was buoyant, 'proof' of the curse lifting having given everyone cause for hope of future love matches.

"So when's the wedding?" Fenella asked.

"Oh, we've not thought that far ahead yet." Callie started fidgeting with her engagement ring.

"You want to get it booked and make sure you're the first bride since the curse lifted. Otherwise, one of those jealous girls will marry any old asshat to beat you down the aisle."

"That doesn't bother me," Callie said, but I could tell by the look on her face that it did. Miss Fake-Fiancée was enjoying the attention.

Served her right for friend-zoning me, otherwise I'd have offered to fake-marry her.

My phone rang, and I stepped out of the room to answer it.

"Lawrence Letwine, you utter bastard," Bernard snapped down the phone. "Get here right now. You're in big trouble with Aria for not telling us your news first. And because of that I'm in big trouble with Aria, so here. *Now.* And bring the fiancée."

There was no way I was taking Callie. We'd have to be brainwashed again and I wasn't in a hurry to repeat last night's antics... Okay I totally would be, but Callie definitely wouldn't.

I stepped back into the room and took Mya's arm, pulling her to one side. "Can you watch Callie for an hour or so? I have to pop back to the mansion."

"Is everything okay?"

"My best friend has just found out I'm engaged and has demanded my presence."

"Oh. Do you need me to enthral you again?"

"Certainly not. Bernard is my best friend, and I will tell him the truth."

"Well, you know best." Mya sighed, intimating I was wrong.

But I did know best, and I also knew that telling Bernard I was in love with Callie didn't require any brainwashing, seeing as it was now becoming clear to me that it was the darn truth.

CHAPTER FIFTEEN

Callie

I'd had so many different emotions over the last three days that I'd just given up now and decided to 'live in the moment'. Tonight, I'd been looking forward to getting everyone into doing this Christmas book read and then when it had actually come down to it, I hadn't cared. Instead, I'd been completely immersed in the bubble where I was engaged, and people oohed and aahed over my ring. I'd seen envy in some women's faces and sheer happiness in others that I'd found my one, and I'd enjoyed the experience so much I'd basically convinced myself just for that hour-and-a-half that I was genuinely engaged and in love. Stepping outside that situation now as people said goodbye and began to leave the room, was bittersweet. The reality of my true situation crept back in, and yet I couldn't regret having enjoyed that moment. If I was living my last days on earth, then that had been a fun experience.

Mya came to my side and smiled. "Lawrie got called back to the Letwine Mansion, so you're stuck with me for a while. I say we go to the bar."

I nodded. A couple of glasses of red wine would go down a treat right now.

"Is everything okay? With Lawrie, I mean," I asked.

"Yes. His bestie just found out about his engagement, so he'll currently be being interrogated. But it's okay. He has it handled. Just someone else who'll know the truth, that's all."

"Right."

We made our way out of the building and headed back towards the village boulevard where the *Smokin' Hot* bistro was.

"Did you enjoy showing off that very impressive rock on your finger?" Mya quizzed.

I grinned. "I really did. Fake engagement and relationship or not, being engaged is fun, and I'm making the most of it. And now we're having a party in Gnarly. I do feel guilty though because people felt it was proof that the curse was lifted, but it wasn't.

What if it's not actually lifted at all, and we're giving villagers false hope?"

Mya shook her head. "It's lifted. Now, don't shout at me, but..." Her words trailed off.

"But what?" I frowned.

"Do you think you might be enjoying your engagement not just because you have a big blingy diamond, but because secretly you do actually like Lawrence?"

My intake of breath was so sharp I was surprised I wasn't bleeding out.

"Absolutely not. He's an idiot. An absolute cock."

"Who you did agree to date once upon a time even though it went wrong. And I did get the gossip off Edmond about that evening, and apparently it was a female vampire with a grudge against him that caused it all."

"I know all about Imelda, but if he hadn't led her a merry dance, she wouldn't have felt the need for revenge would she? I feel sorry for her. Lawrie should not have treated her that way."

"Have you treated all your exes well, Callie?" Mya folded her arms over her chest, waiting for my response.

I thought back and remembered a few things I'd rather have not recalled.

"Apart from when I was young and foolish."

We approached the bar, and I was glad of the reprieve because Mya didn't need to know that I'd once sent a fake VD letter to an ex that I'd bought from a seaside joke shop. Unaware that said ex's father had the same initials, he'd known it was me and we'd had a very uncomfortable confrontation afterwards where I'd been informed I'd caused a lot of trouble between his parents; his mother having thought it genuine and for his dad.

Yes, Mya didn't need to be privy to that ammunition. Then I caught her smiling at me.

"I told you I'm supercharged. However, it hurts my head to break through your guard, so I won't be doing it often. But, Callie, you naughty, naughty girl. And look what happened, your ex came out for revenge. Funny that."

"Oh piss off, and stay out of my head, woman. Get to the bar. I might as well have a bottle of Merlot. Let's not pretend I'm going to stick to one drink tonight."

The bistro was all ambient lighting and mirrored walls, and the bar area had high, small circular tables and matching high, chrome-coloured bar stools with black cushioned seats. The place smelled of cooked meats and barbecue sauce, and wait staff rushed around with sizzling orders for the customers in the eating section.

Mya returned to our table and placed the drinks down. I grabbed the bottle and filled my wine glass almost to the top. Mya's eyes widened.

"So how was dealing with the wayward today?" I asked her, changing the subject.

"Fine. I had one today who arrived with someone's nuts in her mouth."

My jaw dropped. "What the actual…?"

Mya giggled. "Your face. No, this woman had been at a party and had been snacking on a bowl of mixed nuts. She'd got some stuck between her teeth and moaned about it all night. It ended up with her and the party host in a row where she'd thrown the bowl at the hostess' head and accidentally killed her. She came to me because having anything stuck between your teeth is the work of the devil. When I looked at the footage, she'd tried to throw the bowl out of the window, but the hostess had changed direction. Not being able to live with herself, she'd then ended her life. I sent this one upstairs."

"Does this not weigh you down, having fate in your hands and hearing all these awful stories?"

"It's who I am now. And if not, I'd have been a nothingness on the Field of the Drained. No heaven, no hell, just nothing. Dealing with these people reminds me every day of how fortunate I am to have an existence where, like now, I can have a drink with my bestie. Oh shit," she said as she realised I was days away from the end of my own existence.

"Don't worry about it. I realised tonight, while I enjoyed being engaged for a while, that I just can't dwell on dying too much. If I do, I'll waste what time I have left, and who knows, maybe we will save me." I gave a smile, but I knew it didn't reach my eyes. Mya reached across and squeezed my hand.

"I will do everything I can, and Lawrie will too."

"I know. Anyway, I intend to enjoy my engagement. I'm going to enjoy the party, and I'm going to ask Lawrie if he'll take me to Edinburgh because he can whizz me there. There are just a few things I've always wanted to do, and my fake fiancé may as well prove himself useful."

Mya opened her mouth to speak and then closed it again. Then she sighed and spoke. "I know you don't want to hear this. You want to keep Lawrie at a distance, I can see that. I guess because he hurt your feelings before... but Lawrie likes you, Callie. It's very clear to me. The man who pursued you for a date and then kept up banter with you... it's like the mean boy in class who does it because he actually likes the girl but doesn't know how to show it. He didn't need to keep coming back to Gnarly. All this pretence about the Letwine vampires loving your cupcakes. They are amazing, but they sell cupcakes everywhere, especially in London where he actually lives. Plus, let's face it, vampires desire blood, not a moist sponge."

I let myself think about what she said. Was this true? Had Lawrie kept coming to Callie's Cupcakes to see me? Even though I was obnoxious to him every time, and even though he said things that wound me up?

"If he truly disliked you, why would he be trying to save your life? I know he's been told to get a consort, and this delays it, but I've been watching him, Callie, and he never takes his eyes off you."

"Have you spoken to him about what you've seen?"

"Have I fuck. This is Lawrie. He'd tell me I was psychologically disturbed and threaten to stake me with the heel of my favourite Louboutin. Then he'd run, and that would leave you vulnerable." She took a drink of her wine, which looked extremely thick bodied.

"Is that real blood?"

"Yup. I just asked the bartender for an extra glass seeing as you had a whole bottle of red and then I swiftly decanted a pouch."

"So weird."

"Really? You eat the meat of animals but my drinking the blood from them is weird?"

"Huh. I never thought of it like that."

"Me neither before I became a vampire."

Mya launched into a conversation of her discoveries of life as a vampire and it just made me think of Lawrie even more. As the wine flowed ever more freely down my throat, I became more convinced that I was going to throw caution to the wind and have as much fun as possible in my remaining days.

"What else can I do, other than visit Edinburgh?" I asked Mya.

"Nope, you have to think of the things you want to do, so go on, what are your dreams?"

"I always wanted to be kissed in the pouring rain."

"Like in the movies? All romantic. That's a good one. Okay, what else?"

"I think that's it. I want to see Edinburgh, be kissed in the rain, and just live in the moment. I got engaged and that's more than some people, even if it wasn't real."

"Well, I believe his feelings for you are real, even if they're not reciprocated. So you have that too. You were admired, wanted."

My stomach flipped at Mya's words and my heart beat faster.

The bistro door opened and the man himself walked in. I blamed the wine but all I saw was this dashing, sexy man come stalking over to me. "Sorry about that, Callie. I'm back now. Thank you, Mya, you can go now. I'll take it from here."

My glazed eyes saw the look that passed from Lawrie to Mya. The 'you can go now' was backed with a most definite intonation of 'sod off immediately'.

Mya smiled at me in that knowing way. "I rest my case," she said to me. "Goodnight, Callie. Thanks for a great night."

Sadness hit me because usually that would be followed with a 'we must do it again soon'. Though I guessed as most people didn't know when they'd die, in some ways I was fortunate to know what time I had left. To waste any of it would therefore be criminal.

"Do you want me to get you another drink, Callie, or do you have enough left?"

I stared down at my glass. There was half a glass left.

"I want you to take me home, Lawrie. To bed. I want you to fuck me. All night long," I told him. "Make the earth move, fireworks explode. The whole shebang."

Lawrie froze for a moment as if he was still processing my words and then he knocked the glass onto the floor. "Whoops, might as well get straight out of here now," he announced.

Then he whizzed us home.

CHAPTER SIXTEEN

Lawrie

Earlier that evening...

I stood outside my best friend's quarters having knocked on the door to their suite. The door opened and Aria stood there, a hand cocked on her hip.

"You have some explaining to do, Lawrence Letwine. Come inside and sit down in the living room ready for my interrogation. I'll just be getting us some drinks."

Bernard snorted at me as I walked into the room. "Oh you're in so much trouble with my wife, my friend."

"I don't see how. It was all her idea."

Aria walked in at that point carrying a tray with

three glasses of scotch on it. She offered one to Bernard and then to me, before placing the tray down on an ornate marble topped coffee table with a gilt edge and then picking up her own glass.

"I was most perturbed, Lawrie, after being a true friend to you and being on Team Callrence in the past, to find you're engaged to the lady in question without you coming and telling us, or even better, bringing her with you. And then I find you both had dinner with Edmond; although Mya and Death were there, so maybe it was better that we weren't present at that get-together. Still, I have to say it has stung a little, after all the advice I gave you when you were pursuing her." Aria stared at me.

"But it was all your idea to get a fake-fiancée, so I don't understand why you're so pissed off with me."

Aria's jaw dropped. "Your engagement to Callie is fake?"

"Yes. You told me to get a fake fiancée and when I got to Gnarly, Mya let me know that Callie needed a bodyguard and so we made a deal. I would be her bodyguard, and she would be my fiancée."

"No!" Aria cried. "It can't be fake. It can't. I was so happy for you. I thought you'd sorted things out at long last like I knew one day you would, and you'd found your happy-forever-after."

Bernard and I watched as Aria held her hand to her chest and then wiped a red tear from her lower lashes. Dramatic much?

She held up a hand. "It's okay. In the book I read they went from fake to real. So it's fine. Both of your true feelings will emerge through the pretence. There'll be a point where you fall out and it will seem like it's all over and then something else will occur to make you realise you're each other's forever."

Bernard walked over to the sofa, reached behind a cushion and pulled out a Kindle. Then he dashed to the window where he promptly threw it out.

Aria flashed her fangs. "You will pay for that, husband."

"Needs must. You are so wrapped up in that fantasy world, it is interfering in real life." He turned to me. "Yesterday she brought me home a cowboy hat and an axe, saying that she'd been reading about cowboys and lumberjacks. I am magnificent as I am. I do not pretend to be a lesser, *mortal* man." He sneered at his wife.

"If you don't retrieve my Kindle and get those items out of the charity bag you put them in, there will be no more sexy times and I will call you

Bernard the English way forever more. And forevers are a long, long time, Bernie babe."

His jaw set and he looked at me, rolling his eyes. "Be glad yours is fake, mate. Because this is the reality. You lose every argument, all because we have a penis to be blackmailed with." Bernard left the room, I presumed to retrieve all the items.

"Tonight, I will make him chop down trees and ride a horse and then I shall retire with my Kindle and leave him with a hurting right arm and arse. He shall think he has spent time in a male prison when I'm done with him."

I gulped. "Erm, so what's my punishment?"

"I have not decided. You are an imbecile. I meant for you to get a fake fiancée who you didn't care about. Now things shall be complicated when she no longer needs you to be her bodyguard and ditches you again. Why does she need protection anyway?"

"She's going to be murdered on Christmas Eve."

It took a lot to shut Aria up, but that did the trick.

I spent the next few minutes getting Aria and Bernard (who had now returned) up to speed on current events, including being summoned by Edmond and having no choice but to attend and have Mya brainwash us.

"I think mine didn't wear off properly," I confessed.

"What do you mean?" Bernard asked.

"This is why I told you that you are an imbecile. You've fallen for her, haven't you? For real." Aria sighed.

"I may have realised I'm in love with her. Unless it's the brainwashing."

Aria shook her head. "It's not the brainwashing. You've been in love with her since the first moment you saw her. Love at first sight." She gave Bernard a warning glare. "Do not touch my Kindle. This is not what I've been reading. This is the truth. Look at him. He's all pathetic. Does that lovesick look remind you of anyone?"

Bernard peered at me. "Oh God, he is. He's in love. I looked just like that when I realised I loved you."

"Why are you addressing this in past tense? Looked. Loved. Do you want to join Callie in dying on Christmas Eve?"

"No, my sweet wife. You know I love you just as much today as I did then. For instance, would I say you could buy another ten books for your Kindle this evening if I didn't love you?"

She stared at Bernard as if deciding how many different ways she could torture him, then her face relaxed. "Okay, you're forgiven. Let me go bring the rest of the bottle of scotch." She got up and left the room.

"Take note of that. Books. If Callie likes them, you can get away with anything if you just buy them some more."

"Noted. Although I think I have bigger problems than getting out of my girlfriend's bad books."

"Oh yeah, the fact you're in love and a) she doesn't love you back and b) she's going to die."

"Thanks for the summary. I would have struggled to get my head around it were it not for your short recap of my situation."

Aria returned and filled all our glasses.

"So you're engaged. What now?"

"Now I try to look for anyone who might kill her, and we hope to get past Christmas Eve and that The Book of the Dead changes."

"Mya should not have told her. Callie could have happily carried on as she was until the inevitable happened. Instead, she is with a person she dislikes intensely; a situation compromised by the fact her enemy is madly in love with her. When she dies you shall be devastated, Lawrence."

It was the first time I'd given proper thought to the fact that, Callie: Was. Destined. To. Die.

And I'd left her behind to come to see these two.

"I must go. I would never forgive myself if something happened to her while I wasn't there. By the way, we're having an engagement party on Saturday. I'll make sure you get an invite. It's a joint lifting of the Gnarly curse and engagement thing."

I stood ready to whizz off but faced Aria's wrath.

"I really don't see why you make me leave through the door," I huffed.

"It's called manners, Lawrie."

Bernard bade me a good night and Aria walked me to the door and opened it. "I am here for advice if needed. Me and all the authors I've been reading. Otherwise, I will see you on Saturday at your engagement party. Please give my love to Callie and tell her I look forward to seeing her."

As I walked through the door I almost collided with Imelda.

"Stupid idiot," she said as she dodged me.

"I was coming through the door. Where did you want me to go?"

She turned back around. "That's not why I called you an idiot. It's because you are one. And what is this I hear; that someone has actually betrothed themselves to you? Poor fool."

I couldn't help myself. I spat out, "Yes, so don't bother sending all my exes to the engagement party because she's already seen them and is still marrying me anyway."

Imelda looked confused.

"That's right. It's the girl from the restaurant. So, oh dear, looks like you wasted your time with your revenge plans."

Imelda's eyes flashed red. "You'll get yours, Lawrence Letwine," she said, and then she carried on walking down the hall.

I didn't give Imelda another thought though. My mind was consumed with knowing that Callie was safe. I therefore whizzed myself over to the bistro where I could detect my daughter's scent. As soon as I saw Callie, all my feelings of love came flooding back along with sheer lust. I wanted to clear the restaurant and lay Callie down on the table as my feast.

I dismissed Mya and stood by the table, feeling an emptiness in my chest cavity. Though my heart didn't beat, it had never ached before. This must be unrequited love. And then Callie told me she wanted to fuck me and before she had chance to change her mind, I took her straight to her bedroom.

Callie stripped off all her clothes at haste. In fact, I was truly impressed at the speed in which she did so given she wasn't a vamp.

Before long we were back where we had been the night Mya interrupted us, but this time it was just the two of us.

And we weren't brainwashed.

I wouldn't bite her neck tonight. That was one thing I would want her full, sober consent for. I didn't know what had changed her mind and made her want me, but I was here for it.

I stepped forward and lifted her up and placed her on the bed. Lying at her side, I stroked my hands along her body, making her skin goosebump. That was the great thing about a vampire's touch. The coolness of my own skin combined with the stroking meant it would feel amazing. I caressed her breasts and then moved to between her legs. She was most definitely aroused. My eyes cast down on Callie in the moonlight, her head thrown back and her face wanton with lust. I'd never thought I would see the day when Callie would want me in her bed and as the reality of the situation hit, I realised I couldn't do this. If she wanted me, she would have to ask me when sober. What the hell was happening to me? I was an evil vampire. Where were these morals coming from? I moved my hands back to trailing over her body, knowing the hypnotic rhythm would soon take Callie into slumber instead of ecstasy. Then once she was asleep, I moved to the chair in her bedroom, and I watched her and thought about everything that had happened between us until the dawn broke.

CHAPTER SEVENTEEN

Callie

I woke with a dry mouth, but mainly feeling cold. Then it became apparent to me that the chill factor was because I wasn't wearing any clothes.

Sitting up sharply, I looked beside me in the bed, but Lawrie wasn't there. Hearing the clatter of dishes, I detected he was in the kitchen. What had happened last night? I'd asked him to sleep with me, but all I could remember was his touch on my skin and then I must have fallen asleep.

Goddamn it. I'd wanted him to rock my world and instead he'd rocked me to sleep.

And now he was fixing breakfast. I wanted O's not Cheerios.

One thing I was certain of was it hadn't been the

red wine talking last night. I'd definitely decided that I liked Lawrie enough to have endless sex with him until the day I died. He'd got a great bod and I'd seen his dick was more than adequate. I just needed to get him back in my bed now. Swinging my legs out of the side of the bed, I stood and decided I would freshen myself up in the bathroom and then go find him.

By the time I walked into the kitchen sans clothes and all refreshed, Lawrie had laid the kitchen table with coffee and pastries.

He looked up at me and did a double take. "Erm, Callie, you seem to have forgotten your clothes."

"Is there something wrong with me?" I asked, feeling my face fall in desolation.

Lawrie smiled.

"Callie, if you were dressed, I would want to rip the clothes off your body. However, you wanting to do the same to me is something very new, and until I know why you've had a change of heart, I will not be sleeping with you."

I suddenly felt foolish standing there naked. Until Lawrie took his own clothes off. "Here, this is a first for me. Naked breakfast." He went to take a seat.

"I don't think so. I don't want your meat and two veg on my chair. I'm going to get dressed," I told him, and then I went back to my room and did exactly that.

Once back at the breakfast table, Lawrie poured me a fresh coffee. "What happened last night that suddenly had you desperate for my cock?"

I sighed. "I find you attractive, Lawrie. That's the truth. And since you've been protecting me, you've grown on me. When you walked into the bar last night you looked all dashing and like the hero of the hour, all dark and twisty protector. I figured if these are my last days on earth, I'm done denying my attraction to you, and we should have as much sex as possible."

"I think there's a compliment in there somewhere," he replied.

I decided to change the subject. "When I was speaking to Mya last night, I said I had a couple of things on my 'before I die' list and one was to visit Edinburgh, so would you whizz me there?"

"Of course. We can go tonight after work."

"Thank you. I've always wanted to go."

"And what else is on this list?"

There was no way I was telling him I wanted to be kissed in the rain. He wouldn't get it. He was a man and would be thinking of the practicalities, not the romance.

"Well, that's it really."

"Then I shall make sure it's a beautiful trip," he told me. "Now get your breakfast, we have a business to run."

How he said 'we' made my stomach do a flip. Because I liked it. I liked him running the business with me. I'd liked him being here this morning.

I. Liked. Him.

Oh God.

I *really* liked him.

I bolted my breakfast down so I could get out of the kitchen, because right now I couldn't stand the heat.

The day passed quickly with lots of customers coming in to look at my engagement ring and to congratulate Lawrie and I on our news, and the residents of Gnarly buzzed with excitement as they planned Saturday's festivities and celebrated the 'evidence' of the lifted curse.

I enjoyed the day so much that I almost forgot someone wanted to kill me. Almost. But I couldn't help looking at everyone, even those I knew well, trying to see if they looked at me weirdly when they thought I wasn't looking.

I'd thought I was coping relatively well with the whole 'I'm going to die' thing until I spotted my sister giving me a narrow-eyed gaze from where she was sat in the café with Milly and Tilly. The next thing I knew I'd dragged her from her seat. Luckily, the café was closed to new customers, and I'd been waiting for my sister and friends to leave so I could go to Edinburgh.

Lawrie broke my hold and held me back as my sister rubbed the back of her neck where her clothes had been tightened as I'd grabbed her.

"What the actual fuck, Cal?"

"Don't you 'Cal' me. Why were you looking at me with that disgusted face? Is it you? Are you planning on killing me?"

Her mouth dropped open.

Lawrie dragged me over to a chair and sat me down. "Callie. Calm down. Of course your sister isn't trying to kill you." He turned to her. "You aren't, are you? Or are you jealous I want her, not you?"

"She's not the one I'd bump off out of the two of you."

"Thought so," Lawrie said, bringing up a chair

next to mine and sitting down on it. "Callie, what's got into you?"

"Well, not you," I yelled. Hysteria had truly set in. "You won't sleep with me. I think my sister might be wanting to kill me. I'm going insane, Lawrie. Someone wants to kill me, and I don't know who, and I'm running out of time. In a few days I'm going to die. DIE. I don't want to die. I want to live. I have so much still to do with my life."

I burst into tears.

Arms folded around me. Both from my sister and Lawrie and I heard the door open and close. The twins had left. Escorted up to the living room, I cried and cried and cried, until exhausted, I passed out on the sofa.

When I woke, my eyes felt like I'd been punched in them. I was on the sofa covered in my throw. Lawrie moved to my side from the chair nearby.

"What time is it?"

"Just after ten pm."

I sat up and rubbed at my eyes. "I made a fool of myself, didn't I? Thank goodness it was just Dela. I must apologise to her."

"Dela and I talked after you fell asleep. She's aware of the stress you're under, and she's not without her own. You're her sister, her family, and she's desperately unhappy about your situation. She was staring at you with narrowed eyes because she was in a daydream where someone was trying to kill you and she was dragging them off you. She feels helpless. Anyway, I told her that one thing she could do was mind the shop tomorrow so that we could spend the whole day in Edinburgh. She phoned someone called Chantelle and she's helping her. So you can rest up tonight and then tomorrow we can go out for the day."

"That's good. I don't want to go anywhere looking like this."

"Callie, you look beautiful to me, even with puffed up eyes."

I huff-laughed. "Of course I do. You can quit the pretence now, Lawrie. It's just me and you. You don't have to fake love me now."

"What if it's not fake?"

My heart stopped beating.

"Wh- what did you just say?"

Lawrie looked like he wanted to nail his own mouth shut.

"Erm, n- nothing."

"You just said 'what if it's not fake'. Lawrie, what are you saying?"

"Oh for heaven's sake. Okay. You got me. I love

you, all right? Even though you don't feel the same way and you're only with me so I can protect you, my feelings have taken over my common sense, and I love you."

In terms of romance his declaration wasn't exactly my dream. However, it was Lawrie, and this was nothing short of a miracle.

Leaning over to him, I brought my face within inches of his. "I don't hate you anymore," I told him, and then I closed the gap and kissed him.

And this time when he took me to bed, he didn't deny me what I'd been wanting.

The next time I woke, there was a delicious ache between my thighs, and a vampire. I'd woken because Lawrie was busy.

Closing my eyes again, I took in the sensations as he licked and nipped between my legs and then as the pleasure built, he bit me there. I'd never come like it. It shook my body like a level 9 earthquake on the Richter Scale. If he kept on like this, Christmas Eve would be a miracle. I think I'd die of happiness before that. I guessed the meme I'd seen last week on the internet was right. You couldn't have happiness without penis.

After we'd done the deed a few more times, I laid tucked under his arm. The advantage of a cool-skinned lover was after you'd raised the heat levels, he helped you cool down.

"Dela will be here soon, so I suppose we should get up," I said.

"You want me to get up? I'm so happy to oblige." Lawrie flipped me underneath him.

"While I'd love to go another few rounds, Dela really will be here soon and with her living here, she has a key."

Lawrie sighed. "Very well. I shall rise in a different way to the one I prefer." He kissed my neck and I imagined him biting me there again. My body shivered. "Sorry, I'm making you too cold. Why don't you grab a shower here and I'll quickly whizz back to my quarters and shower there?"

By the time I'd got out of bed and turned the shower on, Lawrie had called to say he was back. Vampire speed was some crazy shit, and I was only thankful that he took his time in the bedroom. I replayed all the sexy times in my mind as I showered myself. I couldn't believe that this was the current situation between Lawrie and myself. He loved me!

Did I love him? I couldn't bring myself to face the truth. I just acknowledged that I didn't hate him now, was happy he was here, and enjoyed his company both in and out of the bedroom. Given I was facing death and getting sex after a long period of forced abstinence, I didn't want to assume I was feeling love when it could just be a reaction to the fact these were probably my final days of breathing.

"Don't have any breakfast. I'll take you for food in Edinburgh," Lawrie said as I came into the living room. He pointed to the coffee table where there was a coffee waiting for me. While I was drinking it Dela and Chantelle arrived, and after a few moments of polite chatter, we excused ourselves and the next thing I knew, I was in Scotland.

"So here we are on the High Street. We'll walk up towards the Castle," Lawrie told me as I leant against the Café Nero he'd appeared outside of. Within a minute, the dizziness had stopped, and I was thankful I seemed to be getting used to vampire travel. "Let's go get you something to eat and then we can take an extra coffee with us while we walk up Lawnmarket and Castle Hill."

We sat inside the café after ordering at the counter.

"Have you been here many times before?"

"Never."

"But you sound so knowledgeable."

"I spent a ton of time on Google maps while you slept," Lawrie confessed, and I burst into laughter.

"Happiness suits you, Callie Francis." This time when Lawrie looked at me, his admiration and love was clear in his gaze, and it took my breath away.

"I know how I die," I told him.

"What? How?" he looked around us as if I must have seen something.

"It's because of how you look at me. It makes me forget to breathe."

A silly grin came over his face and he reached for my hand. When Lawrie had sat opposite me, he'd pulled his chair in and our knees touched.

"You make me vulnerable, Callie, and it's something I struggle with. However, I figured if you're brave enough to live life to the full with what's predicted, then I can spend part of my vampire life doing the same."

"This is amazing and unnerving at the same time. I'm so used to your snark and defensiveness." Since he'd told me he loved me, it seemed Lawrie had decided he wasn't holding back with showing me all his feelings.

"My snark's still there don't worry. But I'm

trying to be who you deserve, Callie. The thing is, when I was turned, I was weak and vulnerable and that made me easy prey. Since then, I vowed I'd never be in that situation again. Plus, my long life meant that I could become attached to people knowing they would leave me. Not many live for the same years that vampires do. The irony that I've fallen in love with a fae who should live for a very long time, yet she faces an early demise is not lost on me."

I squeezed his hand. "Maybe I'm a lesson in life, Lawrie, that you have to let yourself be vulnerable and let people in. Maybe you meet the love of your life after I'm gone and it's because of all this." I shrugged my shoulders.

He shook his head. "No, Callie. I already met the love of my life and I'm sitting facing her, looking at her wearing my ring."

He broke off our contact, slid the ring off my finger, and dropped to one knee.

"This time I'm proposing not because I'm brainwashed but because I mean it. Callie Francis, if fate gives us a second chance; if we change what's in the book, can we give this—us—a proper go and see if we were actually meant to be together all along? Will you marry me?"

Tears slid down my face, both with joy at his words, but also at his quiet voice and his nervous smile. The things that showed me the true unbeating heart of Lawrence Letwine, and the feeling of the breaking of my own, given the likelihood that I had eight days left to live.

But right now I was all in.

"Yes," I said, and Lawrie slid the ring back onto my finger as people in the café clapped around us.

CHAPTER EIGHTEEN

Dela

Working at the café wasn't so bad. It was just if I didn't have to then I could do other things instead, like study the male physique and go shopping. Where Callie liked to run the café so she could be at the heart of Gnarly Fell life, I tried my best to escape it.

It was a great place to live with its small, gorgeous buildings and the park, and its mainly friendly residents. But there was a big wide world out there and I'd not even dipped more than a toe in London when it came to flirting with men. Oh, I didn't want to travel the world to see different architecture or culture, I just wanted to sample as many new males as possible before I decided to settle down. And because I'd wanted to meet my Mr Right before Callie did, I'd put speed dating at a whole other level. It meant I could be quite abrupt with men, but I didn't see the point in time wasting if I knew they weren't the one, though I did quite like to sample the goods before I made a final decision at times.

"I'm so jealous of Callie," Chantelle told me for the seventeenth time that morning. I decided to bite this time and ask her why. I'd known Chantelle since we'd moved to Gnarly just over five years ago. She was a witch, but not allowed to practice without supervision as she kept making mistakes. She'd been banned when she accidentally turned Hettie's husband into a cod when she was trying to order fish and chips, and he'd nearly ended up as a day's special.

"Why?"

"Because Lawrie is absolutely gorgeous and he loves her. Proper loves her. She's the first of Gnarly to find love after the lifting of the curse and I want that. I want what she's got."

"You want Lawrie? I'm not sure I can carry on this conversation. That's my sister's fiancé you're talking about."

"No, silly. I want to fall in love and be proposed

to with a huge diamond engagement ring. Don't you?"

"Nope. The only thing I want to be presented with is a huge dick to do with as I wish." Now my sister had managed to get engaged first after all, I was in no rush to get a ring on my own finger.

"Dela! You are so bad."

"Beats being a good girl any day of the week. Speaking of which, do you fancy a night out soon?"

Chantelle shook her head. "I can't. I need to save up for Christmas."

I groaned. All my friends were saying similar things. It was the same every year. As it approached the season of good will to all men, they all went boring. Personally, I thought it should be good willy to all women, but then I always was contrary according to Callie.

Callie.

My beautiful sister who was going to die.

I busied myself in tidying the counter. My way of dealing with stress was to put my head in the sand. I did it when we found out our parents weren't our parents at all and that we were fae, and I was doing it now. She just couldn't die. I'd be left with no one. Yes, I know it would suck for her too, but at least she'd be dead. I'd be left behind to suffer her loss.

"Chantelle. If anything bad ever happened, like I lost a loved one, would you put a spell on me so I wasn't sad?"

"I can't do that, babe. And I don't mean can't because I'm banned, but it's against the rules. Loss is a part of life. In Wicca we embrace the changes in seasons. Death comes to make way for new life. Just trust that loved ones live on in another realm and one day you'll see them again."

"Damn it."

"Anyway, why are you being so maudlin? Your face will put off the customers, well, all except for that one who hasn't stopped staring at you since you came out from the kitchen."

I followed the direction of where Chantelle had made an imperceptible nod of her head and met the eyes of Stan jnr. He quickly looked away.

"He can stare all he likes. He's a Gnarly resident and therefore not to be dated. I don't shit where I eat."

Chantelle's face pinched tightly. "I should hope not, that would be entirely gross."

"It's an expression, Chan. It means that I won't date someone from Gnarly because if it went wrong, I'd have to face him still because of us living near each other."

"Oh right. Well you can't blame me for taking you literally. You fae folk have some weird customs." She clamped her mouth shut.

"How many more times? I am not going to try to steal your teeth. We send baking to the central HQ who distribute to supermarkets and let people ruin their own teeth."

"Oh, he's coming over. I need to visit the kitchen."

"Why? I've been doing the bak—"

She'd gone and I had to look up to meet Stan jnr's eyes.

"Hey, Stan, what can I get you?"

"I'll have another elf cupcake because I can't pull their legs off and eat them in real life, as much as I'd like to."

"Ohhhh-kayyy." Jesus, the guy should order custard to go with him being a fruitcake. I reached up and selected a cupcake, putting it on a plate. "Anything else?"

"Erm, just to say I've changed my name to Nick now, my middle name, as I was fed up of having the same name as my dad."

"Okay. But why did you have to change yours? You should have made him change his. He's older and won't need it as long."

His brow creased. "Well, he's not going anywhere anytime soon and people kind of know him more as Stan A, if you get my drift."

"I'm sorry, I don't know what you're talking about," I replied.

The crease furrowed further. It was a shame Gnarly men were off the table as Nick was fit AF. I reckoned he could lift me with one arm.

Nick leaned in and whispered, "With him being Santa, aka Father Christmas."

I burst out into hearty guffaws. "Oh, you were making a joke. Sorry. I'm going through a bit of an emotional time and so I didn't get it. Yeah, it's funny that Stan A mixed up spells Santa, but then as I keep saying to people, it also spells Satan, and I've heard your dad can be a devil with the ladies."

"No, I—"

I turned to look at the doorway where a group of four women had just come in. Thrusting the plate towards him, I smiled. "Here, on the house to celebrate your new name."

He smiled back. "Funnily enough your sister did something similar when I told her."

"Did she? In that case that'll be £2.99."

He laughed until he realised I wasn't joking. My

sister was running a business, not a charity for Gnarly residents who changed their names.

He paid up and then went to sit back down with his cupcake and I carried on with serving the customers.

Chantelle left an hour before closing and before long there was only me and Nick left. He'd bought a Coke followed by a coffee. As he came back to the counter with his cup and plate, I noticed he was trembling. I wasn't surprised with the sugar rush.

"Thanks, but you didn't need to do that. I'd have cleared your table."

'It's no problem. So, I w- was w- wondering..."

"Yup?" I answered, waiting for him to order a takeout at a reduced cost. Wouldn't be the first time people had asked. However, we sent all remaining cupcakes to Tooth Fairy HQ, also known as the Sugar Shack.

"...if you'd like to have dinner with me?"

"I would have loved to," I lied. "Only, I'm busy with it being the run up to Christmas."

"Oh, me too. Maybe we could pencil it in for the

new year? My dad needs me as back up at this time of the year."

"But your dad shuts down the shop for Christmas, doesn't he?"

"Yes, because he has all the Christmas presents to deliver."

"You must have a large, extended family if it takes the whole of Christmas," I said. "Unless you're trying to joke that he's Santa again."

Nick sighed. "No, we just have a big family." With that, he walked out of the door, luckily having not got out his phone to 'pencil in a date'. Although as I watched his fine arse walking out of the doorway, I wondered if he'd ever thought of moving out of Gnarly so I could move him off my banned list.

For the next hour I cleaned and tidied so that my sister had nothing to do when she got back home. We'd not spoken about her engagement yet, but I was pleased that she and Lawrie had somehow worked through their past problems and had fallen for each other fast. Callie was a romantic whereas romance made me want to be sick. Give me a crime book any day in place of the nonsense my sister read.

I was just placing a refuse sack in one of the large bins out the back when suddenly I found myself *in* the bin. The lid came down and when I tried to lift it, I couldn't. The smell was disgusting, and terror prickled down my skin at being trapped in this small, smelly, confined space.

I screamed at the top of my lungs and hoped someone heard me before the binmen came around at seven pm.

CHAPTER NINETEEN

Lawrie

I knew I loved Callie by the fact that I also knew there were vampires ready to take the complete piss out of me when they witnessed me loved up and I didn't even care. And for the fact that to give her my undead heart this way meant that in just over a week's time I might end up in a long period of mourning, maybe even booking myself a coffin for respite from a broken undead heart.

But between now and Christmas Eve there were eight beautiful days where we could live and love and that was all I intended to focus on now.

We visited the castle and then went to Holyrood House. We had lunch on Princes Street and then went onto Leith. And the more her face lit up and she smiled, the deeper I fell. Dusk fell as we walked hand in hand back so we could see the castle in the distance and Callie sighed.

"Thank you for today, Lawrie. It has been incredible. Edinburgh itself has been better than I could have envisaged and being proposed to again, even if it did take place in Caffé Nero, was absolutely perfect."

Well it wasn't, because while she'd loved the proposal, she was right. Caffé Nero wasn't exactly the thing you wanted to tell your children. Then I remembered she wouldn't be telling any children because a) she was going to die and b) vampire/fae babies were a rare occurrence anyway. But I could still do better and so I grabbed her and spirited her away until we appeared on the top of Arthur's Seat. Callie once again was sans engagement ring and had this vampire on one knee in front of her. I gave her a few minutes to orientate herself.

"Callie Francis. While you have this beautiful scenery around you, with 360-degree views of Edinburgh in the evening, I ask for you to become my wedded wife. I love you. Will you marry me?"

She dropped to her own knees. "Yes. Absolutely yes. I- I love you too."

I still couldn't believe my ears after how much

she had seemed to despise me in the past. I brought my lips to hers in a soft kiss and slipped the ring on her finger once more.

"Thank you for doing that. I've had the most amazing proposals now," she said as we stood. I came behind her and wrapped her in my arms as we looked out over the city.

"Marry me right now, Callie," I said. "What are we waiting for? We want to be together. Let's do this. We can stay in Scotland and go to Gretna Green." I'd never felt more sure of anything in my life. I wanted to make her my wife, so that even if I lost her, for a moment we'd found each other.

I felt her startle and heard her breath catch. She turned in my arms and looked up at me, hooking a hand in a belt loop on my trousers, pulling me closer. Her cheeks were as pink as her hair.

"I want to say yes, but I can't get married without my sister being there, Lawrie. She's everything to me and I would want her there. And Mya, my best friend and your daughter. What about Bernard and Aria too? Would Aria forgive you if she wasn't there?"

I sighed. "You make a fair point. So how about we go get your sister right now, and then I'll call

Mya, plus Bernard and Aria and we can head straight back?"

"Perfect," she said.

Leaving the beauty of Edinburgh behind us, we whizzed back to Gnarly Fell to collect our wedding guests.

I brought us back to the café but there was no sign of Dela. Callie scowled as she looked around and went into the kitchen. "Great. She must have decided she was bored of tidying up and so went home. Typical Dela."

But I could hear what Callie couldn't. I dashed through the door out the back which I realised was still unlocked and followed the sounds of Dela's screams for help. Lifting the lid of the bin, I recoiled at the smell as I quickly pulled Dela out of it.

She was hysterical. "Oh my god. Thank you, Lawrie. I am so pleased to see you. I never thought I'd say that sentence, but, oh fuck it." She threw her arms around me, and I could feel the wetness from her cheek touch my own. Christ, she stank.

Callie had come outside and frozen mid-movement. "Wh- wh- what. Oh God." She ran forward and Dela slipped from my arms into Callie's.

"I thought I was going to die. The binmen would have been here soon."

"They thought you were me," Callie said as she looked at Dela. "The hairnet covers your hair. They clearly thought you were me. They tried to kill me." She looked at me over her sister's shoulder. "Why was this not in The Book of the Dead? Mya would have told me."

"Because this isn't when you die. It's an attempt that went wrong. Therefore, it's not in the book. It's awful, but Dela wasn't fated to die tonight."

"Oh, of course. Lawrie, thank God you have super-hearing. I would have just thought she'd left. Oh, Della, I'm so very sorry."

They hugged each other tighter, and I realised that the epic romantic moment of us speeding off to get married tomorrow had passed. I sagged against the back wall of the café as the sisters continued to hug and then Callie instructed her sister to go upstairs and get a bath or shower while she made some sweet tea.

Once Dela was in the shower, I approached Callie. "I'll be nearby. I'll go sit downstairs probably. But you and your sister need tonight together. I'll not go in your room in case you decide to bunk up for the night if she doesn't feel safe."

Callie leaned back and crinkled her eyes at me. "Not one comment about asking if you could watch. You truly are a changed man, Lawrence Letwine. I'm sorry about our plans. Just didn't seem right given the circumstances."

"It's fine. Let's have a quiet day tomorrow and then enjoy the party Saturday and take it from there." I went in my pocket. "I found this stuck to the top of the bin before I opened it." I handed Callie the piece of paper.

In the dustbin where you belong like the trash you are.
Lawrie will 'refuse' to marry you when I'm finished.

Her eyes dulled and she gave a half-hearted shrug. "Still no clue as to who it is. That could be equally someone from Gnarly jealous I'm now engaged, or one of your admirers."

All of a sudden, I figured I knew who it might be. The one person who'd tried to get in the way of our relationship before, and who'd threatened me again just recently. Imelda. I'd have to speak to Mya about her keeping an eye on Callie again tomorrow while I paid the woman a visit.

But for now, I was staying by my fiancée's side. Not literally of course. Tonight, that place would be filled by Dela. I swiftly kissed her lips. "Just call out if you need me. I'll go finish tidying the café and prepare for tomorrow, and I'll open up if needed."

"I'm sorry for the time I hated on you, Lawrie," Callie said, her fingers trailing down my cheek.

"Don't be. It was fun at times. Let's call it foreplay." I winked at her and then I was gone.

CHAPTER TWENTY

Callie

I changed my mind about sweet tea and made Dela a sweet hot chocolate instead with whipped cream and marshmallows.

When she emerged from the bathroom, she was dressed in a pair of my comfy pyjamas, and I handed her my throw to wrap around herself. We sat near each other on the sofa.

"Fuck, Callie. That was a real near miss tonight." Her lip trembled as she spoke. "And it makes it so real that you might actually die." At that point she burst into tears. All I could do was hold her until she'd finished sobbing and then I handed her a tissue. When she'd dried her eyes and blown her nose, I passed her the now not-so-hot chocolate.

"How can you cope, knowing someone is

wanting to kill you?" Dela asked me, moving closer and squeezing my hand.

"It just doesn't seem real to be honest with you, Dela. I think over the past few days I've been upset, angry, and I've settled into a place where I'm looking around myself all the time for unusual activity, but at the same time it's like I don't believe it. Plus, the fact it's scheduled for Christmas Eve means I kind of don't need to worry about it right now. Well, I didn't think so until tonight where now I realise that the person can still attempt to kill me, even though they don't succeed until the 24th."

"This really sucks." Dela sighed.

"So does my vampire boyfriend," I quipped.

Dela's eyes widened for a moment and then we both burst out laughing.

"Come on. Pick a feel-good movie and let's curl up and watch that. Then you can come sleep in my bed. I'll change the sheets," I hastened to add.

"Thanks, sis. I'll be okay tomorrow. It's just the thought of being in that small, stinky space, thinking that at any moment I might be crushed to death." She shivered.

"I know." I showed her the note then and how I just had no clue as to who could be behind it.

"Before we watch the movie, tell me about your day," she said. So I did.

"You were coming back to get me and to get married? Oooh, if we find who's trying to kill you, I shall kill them first. They spoiled it. We can still do that. Tomorrow we could all go to Gretna Green."

I shook my head. "The moment passed. Now I'm focusing on the party in Gnarly that's also our engagement party and then who knows, maybe when it's finished, we can go to Scotland afterwards?"

"That would be lovely. Now is there anything I can do to make the celebrations on Saturday the ones of your dreams?"

"Just be there, Dela. As the only family I have here, just be there."

"Do you think about any of them?" she asked quietly. "Either our human parents or our fae ones."

"Sometimes. But I try not to. They're all in the past, and I'm focused on the future. Or should I say, I was. Now I potentially don't have much of one."

"Perhaps you could reach out and let them know?"

I shook my head. "No, Dela. They haven't made any attempt to contact us since we left. They could have missed marriages, and babies. They've missed birthdays. I'm not having my final days in false reunions where they'll give out sympathy regardless of their true feelings, or still not want us and reject us. However," I took a breath. "If you want to get in touch with them again that's fine with me. You're your own person. All I ask is you wait until I've gone because I don't want to see them."

"I understand," she said.

Then she chose a film to watch, and we settled down to laugh at *The Proposal* while we ogled Ryan Reynolds. The shock seemed to morph into exhaustion and after the credits rolled, we went to bed and both fell straight to sleep.

By the next morning Dela seemed much more herself. "My near-death experience has showed me that I need to live life with no regrets, so I'm going to go set up some more dates and make sure to enjoy myself. I'll see you at the party tomorrow. I wonder if anyone on Tinder will miraculously look like Ryan Reynolds?"

"I thought I was the one hoping for a miracle," I replied.

After getting ready, we went downstairs, and my

stomach burst with the feeling of butterflies as I pushed open the door to the café. Only to find Mya there and no sign of my fiancé.

"Oh."

"Thanks a lot. Here I am minding your caff and protecting you and you look at me with crushing disappointment."

"Sorry."

"Is it because you're in lurve?"

"She's sickeningly in love," Dela answered. "But I'll put up with it seeing as she's also fated to die."

"Gee, thanks."

"You're welcome. Anyway, thanks for last night. I know how hard it must have been to tear yourself away from your new fiancé's penis when time is running out on that particular ride. I'm off to find my own joystick. See you tomorrow."

With that Dela left.

"So where is Lawrie?" I asked.

"He had some urgent business to attend to at the Letwine Mansion, so I said I'd come here as the wayward can wait. I've set a couple of them up in time loops so that by the time I get back they'll have seen the error of their ways."

"Appreciate it. Still no change in my fortunes then?"

"'Fraid not."

"Thought as much," I said bleakly as I headed into the kitchen to start putting buns in the oven. Mya followed me in there. "I'm up to speed on everything that's happened, both the good and the bad. Sorry you weren't able to get married."

I shrugged my shoulders. "It is what it is. I still think I'm dreaming you know?" I confessed. "Sometimes I just stand still and I think about my foretold death and that I'm in love and engaged to Lawrie, and I think this cannot be happening."

"We all think that when our circumstances quickly change. I still have periods like that now myself."

"Do you miss your old life?"

"Not really. Sometimes I miss the bookstore. I liked matching people up with reads. Some would come back and thank me and then buy more by that author and it felt good."

"Then why not open up the library?"

"I can't really run it around the wayward. I never know when I'll be called to deal with a spirit. Plus, I don't think purgatory is the best place for gnarly residents to visit."

"If I wasn't about to die, I'd convert this place and make it *Books and Buns*," I told her. "I've often thought of extending the building. The truth is, Callie's Cupcakes will probably be no more." Tears filled my eyes and Mya came and put her arm around me. "Dela won't continue it. She's never been that interested."

"Callie, we're closing the café today," Mya announced. "Once those buns have cooked, we're off shopping. The place will be closed tomorrow, so what's one more day? Like you say, soon the place will be no longer and so Gnarly residents will have to find some other way to satisfy their sweet tooth. We're going to buy killer outfits for tomorrow and sexy lingerie for tomorrow night. Time to have some fun."

"Okay." The idea of sexy lingerie and a beautiful outfit for tomorrow appealed, and I had plenty of money, so I wasn't worrying about how much I spent.

"You keep an eye on the buns and I'll go make a notice for the window in the café door," Mya ordered.

When she'd gone, I sent Lawrie a text explaining I was going shopping with Mya and not opening the café, but he didn't reply. I wondered what business he'd had to go to the mansion for and hoped everything was okay.

CHAPTER TWENTY-ONE

Lawrie

Once I'd decided it was Imelda, my true vampire nature had descended. All I could think of was tearing her limb from limb. But vampires liked to torment their prey first, even if it was another vampire, and I would make Imelda regret ever having interfered with Callie's life.

I went to The Vampire's In(n) and walked straight over to the bar where Virginia was looking bored in the company of the patron sitting in front of her. "Lawrie." Her eyes brightened and she looked pleased to see me which I think meant more from my rescue of her from the drinking patron than of actually having her brother walk in.

"So I hear congratulations are in order, brother

dearest. I look forward to meeting the one who has managed to tame you, and a fae too." She poured me a straight O-neg which was perfect. It would strengthen my killer instinct for when I found Imelda.

"There's an engagement party tomorrow in Gnarly if you want to come."

"I suppose I should attend as family," she said.

"Don't show too much enthusiasm," I retorted.

"You've always told me how weird and dull it is there!"

I looked at my feet. "I may have not wanted to admit how much I liked Callie and so diminished the pleasure I got from attending there."

"In that case, why are you here?"

"I have some business to attend to with Imelda. Have you seen her?"

"Most of the women are dressing the two huge Christmas trees that were delivered this morning and are around the entrance of the mansion."

"Thanks. I'll check."

"Are you going to tell me why you need to see her? Is there unfinished business between you two? I know you dated before, but after she sent all your snacks to that restaurant, I thought you'd not spoken."

My fangs descended, despite my trying to keep my cool.

"Whoa. She's pissed you off then."

"I spoke with her the other day, and she basically warned me that I would 'get mine' whatever that meant. Yesterday, Callie's sister was mistaken for her and almost ended up crushed in a large rubbish bin and a threatening note was left."

"And you think it's Imelda?"

"She's top of my list of suspects given her past behaviour. Callie certainly has no enemies I know of."

"How do you know it's not one of your snacks?"

I laughed. "As if humans would take on vampires and fae outside of a work of fiction."

"They could have teamed up with a paranormal?"

"True, and that would once again lead me back to Imelda. So, I'm going to go *ask*."

Before my sister could say anything else I'd gone.

⬩

Imelda was indeed part of the ensemble dressing the tree. How very tedious, I thought as they passed baubles along a row up the stairs until one leaned over to fix it in place. Then they'd deliberate over if it was in the perfect spot. And then after all that they insisted on matching the second tree to the first, so it looked like a mirror image. They could fly up and have it done in an hour, but always wanted to make a 'thing' of it.

I walked in and passed them all, going up the staircase, and as I walked past Imelda, I mouthed, 'Ugly bitch' at her. One thing I was sure of. Imelda thought she was the most beautiful female vampire of them all. The wicked witch in Snow White had nothing on her.

As I got halfway down the hall, Imelda flew at me, but I was ready.

I grabbed her by the hair, opened the ballroom door, and threw her at the wall. She hit the floor, played dead for a few seconds and then came back, drop kicking me in the side of the head.

"Fuck." I rubbed at my sore ear.

Back upright and at close distance, I lifted up my leg, aiming to kick her straight in her stupid pouty lips. Instead, I found myself held back by Edmond, and Imelda restrained by Davinia.

My sister entered the room. "Sorry, bro. Couldn't let you do something you'd regret. You're in love with Callie so hard you're prepared to go into battle for her, but by doing so you could ruin your future together."

"No one breathes a word of this to Radaya or anyone else on the council, you hear me?" Edmond spat out.

"Agreed. The last thing we need is to sit in a boring council meeting just before Christmas," Davinia seconded.

"So, what happens in this room stays in this room and to that end, we will let you both go now, and you will sit on the floor cross-legged like the small children you're behaving like until I know the truth," Edmond ordered.

"Perfect," I yelled. "Because you can read her mind and discover that she's trying to kill my fiancée because she's so bloody jealous of her."

"Jealous? I feel sorry for the poor cow."

"Davinia. Silence her," Edmond commanded.

Davinia only had to stare at Imelda with her cold, dead eyes and she shut right up.

Both of us sat cross-legged. I'd endure any humiliation if it meant that it saved Callie's life. After this we would be free to love each other for eternity.

Edmond knelt in front of a trembling Imelda and compelled her.

"Imelda de Costa. Have you been trying to kill or

wound Callie Francis or cause any evil intent to Lawrence?'

Imelda's eyes glazed over and turned black. Here it came. Her confession.

"No. I have not."

"Liar," I shouted and found myself compelled to not speak by the elder.

"Please state your intentions towards Lawrence Letwine."

"I despise the man because I was once stupid enough to go on a date with him. All he talked about was himself. Then when I made a date with Christian, who I had tried to make jealous by agreeing to a date with Lawrence, this idiot told him I was as entertaining as trying to light a wet bonfire and not to bother. So Christian cancelled our date. In retaliation I ruined Lawrie's date with the fae woman."

"And since then?" Edmond prompted.

"Since then I have avoided Lawrence as much as possible. Indeed, until the other evening, I'd managed to barely come across him. Largely because he's usually aware of no one else's existence but his own."

"And then you threatened him, right?" Virginia said. It was good my sister had my back seeing as I couldn't speak.

"I couldn't help myself. I bumped into him because he wasn't looking where he was going, and he blamed me. I told him he'd get his, which he will. One day he'll piss someone off too much and they'll stake him."

"So what you are saying is that you dislike him intensely, but you do not intend to harm him or Callie?" Edmond surmised.

"Indeed. I have better things to do with my time, like continue to try to get Christian to notice me."

"You may remove the thrall, Davinia," Edmond commanded, and he took away my muteness.

"But if it's not Imelda, who is trying to kill my fiancée?" I said, placing my head in my hands.

Edmond actually slipped an arm around me.

"Lawrence. I am sorry to hear of this. But if you suspect any other vampires you must come to me and I will investigate. There will be no more confrontations like this. Do you understand?"

I looked up. "Yes. I am sorry." My eyes flitted to my sister. "Thank you. I almost made the worst mistake of my life, taking myself away from my love." I got up to leave. "I must return to protect my fiancée. I apologise to you, Imelda, and before I go, I will attempt to make amends and talk with Christian."

She nodded.

I walked out of the building with my sister. "Christian will be in the bar by now, brother. Let's go see him and then you can go back to Callie."

So a vampire walked into a bar, and he sought out a fellow vampire and confessed to having had spoken ill of Imelda in the past.

"So you may want to take her out on a date."

"You and Imelda might like to look outside of yourselves now and again. Because if you did, you might notice that I've been dating Johan Danes for the last decade." He rolled his eyes.

"Oh," I remarked, noticing that he did actually have his hand on Johan's thigh.

And as I returned to Callie, I laughed, because Imelda was still a vain bitch, whereas I was finally learning to look outside of myself.

"Any joy?" Mya asked as I arrived back at the café, appearing in the living room where I noticed you could barely move for shopping bags. The brands of some made my loins leap as I recognised them as lingerie shops. It was time for Mya to leave.

"Nothing. False alarm." I sighed. "However, it

looks like joy can still be on my agenda here, so it's good to see you daughter, but now kindly fuck off."

"Such love for your daughter. It must bring a tear to Callie's eye, the emotion." She turned to Callie who was looking at me like I was an ice-cream in a heatwave. "Clearly I'm wasting my words here. See you tomorrow," she said and disappeared.

"I missed you," Callie said.

"I missed you too. I thought I knew who was behind the threats, but alas, I was mistaken."

"The fact you tried I feel deserves a reward." Callie picked up a bag and winked at me. "When I call your name, come get me," she said, skipping out of the door.

I took a moment to allow myself to feel the disappointment and sadness that her attacker was still out there, with another day almost gone, and then I pushed it down deep inside, because we still had tonight.

When she called, I came running, and boy, did I get a reward. Crotchless panties and a peephole bra. If I wasn't already dead, Callie dressed in that outfit would have killed me. And I'd have died with a huge smile on my face too.

CHAPTER TWENTY-TWO

Callie

I stretched out in the bed on a brand-new day, re-living the antics of the night and early morning in my head. My body ached deliciously. I could hear Lawrie moving around in the kitchen and took the moment to think. Because something had come to mind since Dela had been mistakenly attacked, which was that although Mya had told me that I would be murdered on Christmas Eve, it didn't mean that's when I would be attacked. I could be beaten up today and not die until next Saturday, meaning technically I died on Christmas Eve, but in actual fact life could go downhill at any time.

I intended to keep these thoughts to myself. It would only have everyone in my life suffocating me as they became ultra-protective. I'd keep alert myself, but I decided I couldn't face spoiling a day that could be magical, worrying it might be my last one conscious. Today was our engagement party and the Gnarly lift-curse celebrations and I thoroughly intended to enjoy it. And then if after that Lawrie and I decided to elope... well, I'd enjoy that too. And while I could feel a small stone in my gut, a stone of unhappiness that I'd found my happy ever after as 'ever' came closer to fading away; I would push it out of my mind for today at least.

The celebrations began at three pm, but in the meantime Lawrie and I needed to get hot and steamy... in the kitchen. I'd agreed to make lots of cupcakes. They were to be assorted flavours, but I was making all the frosting white as a bridal gown, with pearl button accents, and they'd be wrapped in white lace cases.

The bedroom door pushed open and Lawrie walked in with a piping hot coffee on a tray; a bowl of cubed assorted melon; and some toast, butter, and jam.

I pushed myself further up the bed. "Breakfast in bed. You spoil me."

"As soon as I felt you stir, I thought I may as well make myself useful. I helped expend a lot of your energy the last few hours. Seemed only fair to help you gain some."

"Would you really have married me if we hadn't have found Dela in the dustbin?" I'd begun to wonder if Lawrie had been caught up in the romance of the moment in Edinburgh.

"I'd skip the engagement party and marry you right now," he replied, sitting next to me on the bed. His fingers tipped up my chin, so I was looking in his eyes. "Callie. Let me make this perfectly clear. The fact I pestered you for a date, and continued to pester you after it went wrong, coming to Gnarly for the simple matter of *only* coming into your café to torment you, should have shown the both of us that my feelings had not lessened. I'm sad it took a prediction of your death for me to realise that I am, and always have been, head over heels in love with you. This also should be apparent by the fact I am attending a party where I have to be polite and civil to people. Do you realise how difficult it will be to bury my sarcasm and insults?"

Leaning forward he kissed my lips, just a reassuring brush.

"Now eat and drink up because you committed us to making an unholy amount of buns when we could have been making out instead."

"Let's get married tomorrow," I said, and Lawrie beamed.

"I shall look forward to it. We can do Gretna Green or Las Vegas. You decide. We would also usually have to have a vampire ceremony within the month, but I guess..."

"I have a week. If they can arrange it quickly, I'd love to marry you in an official vampire ceremony."

"What about a Fae one?" he asked.

I shook my head. "No. Dela and I are earth living fae, so we get married like humans. We'd have to apply for the Otherworld and agree to live there for part of the year. It's not something I wish to do. Vegas, however, sounds like a lot of fun!"

Leaning over again to kiss me on the top of the head, Lawrie then shuffled off the bed. "I'll go and preheat the ovens. You enjoy your breakfast and I'll see you downstairs shortly."

He left the room, and I ate my breakfast thinking about the fact not only did I now have an engagement party today, but I was getting married tomorrow.

Gnarly Fell boulevard looked exquisite and mother nature had decided to bless us with a mild December day, with winter sunshine shining through the gnarled trees. Along with the twinkling white lights they'd put up for Christmas, long tables had been set up down the centre of the boulevard with silver tablecloths and vases of red roses. Large, red blooms made from silk and taffeta had been weaved through the trees, so they all looked as if they'd blossomed with ruby roses. At the far end of the boulevard was the large Christmas tree erected every year which carried huge red and green baubles, and red and green large lights.

It looked stunning. Helpers had been to the café earlier and picked up the buns, and all the food was distributed evenly down the centre of the large trestle tables between the vases of roses. We all had a recyclable plate and cutlery at the place where we'd be seated. There was no seating plan, apart from Lawrie and I had been told we would be sat facing each other right in the middle.

We'd got showered and changed after all the heat of the kitchen had spilled out into a bedroom quickie. Lawrie of course was ready within a speedy vampire minute, while I took a little longer. The look in his eyes as he saw me though took my breath away. Such reverence in his gaze, along with lust.

Mya had insisted on this dress when I tried it on. A baby pink satin, it hugged my curves in a bodice shape on top, with just two thin straps. The skirt came out to just above my knee and had a layer of pink lace on top and a white taffeta underskirt. A white lace cardigan completed the look. It was short so it just basically just covered my shoulders. I wore white lace pumps on my feet.

I'd curled my hair, something I did rarely, so it landed in ringlets onto my shoulders, and I had a small white lace headband in my hair. I felt amazing. Happy to be in the spotlight to celebrate with my fellow villagers.

Music played through speakers dotted around the boulevard and Lawrie and I chatted to other villagers until Fenella spoke through a microphone set up on a small stage at the opposite end of the boulevard to the Christmas tree, and asked people to take a seat. Dela sat beside me, with Mya and Death close by, and we were also joined by Bernard and Aria, Lawrie's sister Virginia, and Edmond, who had decided to invite himself, presuming it was a given that he would be there.

"Oh you are so beautiful," Aria exclaimed,

staring at me. I reassured myself that it was admiration and not hunger in her eyes. "I can see why Lawrie is so taken and in love with you. I knew he was in love with you before he did, you know? It does take men a while, but that's because their brains have to move from the penis to their heads. It causes a delay in common sense."

Her husband rubbed at his temples. "Cupcake, my love?" he asked her, taking her mind elsewhere and then occupying her mouth. I couldn't help but smile.

After everyone had eaten, Fenella once more took to the microphone. "Villagers. Right now, our amazing volunteers are coming around to fill the glasses in front of you with champagne. Please could we give our appreciation to not only them, but to everyone who has helped make the celebration a complete success."

We all applauded. Once our glasses were full and Fenella had also been passed one, she raised her glass and said, "A toast. To the engagement of our own Callie Francis who we love dearly, and her new fiancé Lawrence. We welcome the Letwine family officially to Gnarly," she said nodding at our vampire friends. "And also we celebrate the fact that Gnarly has indeed had the curse lifted from it that means like Callie and Lawrie, we might also find our happy ever afters." There were cheers and as I looked around, I noticed that Nick was staring at my sister, who unfortunately for him didn't notice. *Interesting.*

"To Callie and Lawrence. May you experience much joy and happiness in your married life."

"To Callie and Lawrence," the villagers chanted, as we all raised our glasses, and took a drink.

"And to the love lives of Gnarly," Fenella added.

"The love lives of Gnarly," we repeated and then we all took a sip.

It was at that moment, while everyone toasted, clinked glasses, and was blissfully happy that there was a boom as fireworks went up in the park.

"That's not supposed to have happened yet," Fenella shrieked. "Who the hell has set those off?"

We were all looking in the direction of the park while the fireworks emerged into the sky at once. It was only just going dusk and so not only were they not being seen at their best, but it sounded like bombs were going off. Everyone was distracted and I guess that was my enemy's plan, as all of a sudden, I felt someone behind me and the next minute I was gone.

I found myself around the back of my café near to the bins again, in the company of a small woman

I'd never seen before. Given her red eyes and descended fangs I was clear about *what* she was, just not *who* she was. She began to fasten iron chains around my wrists which started a slow burn through my skin. It was agony and I felt faint. I dropped to my knees.

"Ooh, it said it would burn slowly and painfully. Good. That's how Lawrie made me feel," she said. "Do you know he said I wasn't good enough for him because I was fat? He intimated that I'd probably eaten all my dates which was why I was still single. So fixed on looks. And what does he choose for his future bride? Miss Pretty-in-Pink. Well, it's not happening. He can find out what it's like to be pitied once I've killed you."

The intense pain made it hard for me to speak, but I managed to grind out, "Wh- who are y- you?"

"My name is Katerina. But you can call me your murderer."

CHAPTER TWENTY-THREE

Lawrie

One minute Callie was there, the next she wasn't. Panicking, I screamed at Mya, who quickly looked at her The Book of the Dead app. Or rather, she tried to, because the moment she clicked in, I stole the phone from her hands, stared at it and threw it back at her.

It was all there. She would die at the hands of Katerina behind the cupcake café. I could only hope to get there in time.

Appearing at the side of Katerina, she smiled a wicked smile at me, and I saw she had a gun pointed at my fiancée which no doubt contained silver bullets. "Well, well, well, if it isn't the loved-up Lawrie. Let me guess, you've come here to appeal to my better nature and be nice to me now you're forced to be. Well, you can go fuck yourself, because I'm going to kill your fiancée and then watch you suffer."

Two more soft landings put Mya and Death amongst us. At that point I swallowed hard, and I prayed to a God I hadn't believed in since my own life was taken from me. Death was here. He had come for my fiancée. At that point I knew I had to do something quickly.

"Katerina. My daughter, Mya, over there has the power to enthral even the strongest of vampires. If it is acceptable to you, then I will have her take away all of my love for Callie, so that I don't remember ever having loved her. You can take great joy in having robbed me of that love. Or she can even suggest to me that I love only you and you can then keep me at bay, taunting me that I can't have you and letting me live in eternal torture until at such time you decide to stake me."

I made the mistake though of looking back at Callie. The black burn of the iron was seeping up her arms now, slowly poisoning the love of my life.

Katerina's eyebrows lowered and pinched and then she pulled the trigger.

I dived in front of Callie, knocking her out of the way, as Mya tackled Katerina. Then there was an almighty shadow like a black cloud overhead as Edmond appeared. We watched as he drove a stake into Katerina's chest and she turned to dust. I quickly pulled the chains off Callie's wrists and biting my own wrist I held my bleeding wound to her mouth. "Drink."

She did as asked, and as my blood hit her system the black began to recede. I pulled the bullet out of my midriff and watched the wound heal over. Then I gathered her into my arms.

But what happened next shocked us all. Edmond turned around to Death and said, "I'll let you do the honours in explaining what just happened here. Mya, welcome to your lesson of what happens if you give out the secrets of The Book of the Dead."

We all looked from Edmond to Mya and then to Death as he stepped forward and shook Edmond's hand. "Thank you."

Then Edmond was gone.

Katerina's dust sailed up into the air and soon it was like she'd never been there either.

"May we all sit in your living room, Callie, so I can explain how you are still alive?" Death asked.

Callie nodded and sombrely, we all moved to the living room.

Callie still looked a little wide-eyed, but that could have been as much from the blood boost she'd received as from shock. I sat beside her on the sofa, with Dela who had now arrived at her other side, and we squished her between us. Mya was in the seat opposite, and Death stood beside her.

He cleared his throat.

"I was requested by both God and Satan to put Mya to a test to see if she could keep the secrets of The Book of the Dead to herself should they involve someone she knew and cared about."

Mya gasped. "This was a test?"

Death carried on, looking at Callie as he spoke. "I protested vociferously. Not because I didn't feel Mya should be tested, but because I didn't feel it was fair to subject someone to believing they were going to die if they weren't. However, I was overruled by all of the above and below hierarchies and told that all would come to make sense."

"How dare they?" Mya yelled. "How fucking dare they?"

Death held up a hand to silence her. She looked like she wanted to break it, along with several other of his body parts, but she did quieten.

"Therefore, The Book of the Dead foretold Callie's death. If Mya hadn't have told you, Callie, you wouldn't have ended up in the situation you found yourself in. The prediction would have just disappeared from the book the following day.

"However, Mya didn't keep the matter confidential as she knows she has to regardless of whose death it predicts, and she therefore set off a chain of events which led to Katerina attempting to kill you. As The Book of the Dead changed its prediction two hours ago, I told Edmond about the test and about Katerina."

"So Katerina was staked because Mya told me I was going to die?" I queried. I didn't like the woman, but she didn't deserve for her fate to be changed as part of a test.

Death shook his head. "Katerina's death was imminent anyway. Edmond had his suspicions that she'd been killing human men who insulted her appearance. He'd found proof of this just before he came to the celebrations."

"So I caused this from not keeping my mouth

shut?" Mya's eyes filled with tears. "My friend suffered all these days because of me. Because I tried to warn her?"

"It's the human part of you still showing," Death said. "But you have to repress it until your vampire and deathly existence take over, which they will in time. I love you for it, but unfortunately you can't do it, Mya. It's against all the rules."

"Callie, I am so very sorry." Mya wept as she apologised, placing her head in her hands.

"Well don't be, you silly cow," I snapped and her head shot up. "If you hadn't blabbed, I wouldn't be engaged to this man at my side. I'd have still been hating on him, not knowing that he was my protector, someone who was prepared to sacrifice himself for me."

"That's very true," Mya said, wiping at her eyes.

"Now, I think you should listen to Boss man and keep the contents of The Book of the Dead to yourself from now on, because next time things might not work out quite so well, and it might not be a murderous vampire who bites the dust."

Death nodded at me in thanks and then he looked over at Mya.

"This is why you shouldn't date your colleagues,"

she snapped. "It makes it very difficult for you to play nice when they've made you sit a horrible test."

"Don't be too hard on him, Mya. He had no choice, and everything's worked out for the best, hasn't it? Why don't you make him buy you a new outfit for our wedding tomorrow?"

"Eeeeeeek," Mya and Dela shrieked simultaneously. Then Mya looked at Death. "Right, we need to get back, honey, because I'm going to process as many of the damn wayward as I can so that those above and below can find out what it's like when I'm pissed off. Hell can find out there really is no rest for the wicked as all those new souls come through and they can play Eric Clapton upstairs because there really will be Tears in Heaven."

"I much prefer the shopping idea. I have lots of money for you to spend," Death pleaded.

"If that's everything," I said. "I'd like to be left alone now to process what just happened. Lawrie and I will be in touch later with the details of our wedding."

Everyone left after bestowing me with long lasting hugs. I even had one from Death along with another apology.

I knew I was still in shock. I was going to live

until that book predicted my official last day on earth and now, I'd never know about it.

And so therefore I would live every day like it could be my last, and I'd start by marrying the love of my life. After I'd spent all evening showing him my appreciation of his saving my life that was.

EPILOGUE

Callie

I stood in front of an altar in a small chapel in Las Vegas. Elvis was marrying us, and we were all dressed in our finest.

Elvis broke off to look at us all and nodded his head while he went, "Yeahhh! Good to see you folks getting in on the dress up action."

I was dressed in a white version of the dress I'd worn yesterday, but with a white veil in my pink hair, and my faery wings as extra accessories. My groom stood dressed in a tux with a blood red tie and matching eyes. His fangs were in attendance.

My sister was dressed in a pale green bridesmaid dress, also with her gossamer wings on show. She looked like a large scale Tinkerbell.

Mya had chosen a black slinky dress that cut

away to show her leg and also dipped low to show a healthy dose of bosom. She said she was dressed as Elvira, from the movie Elvira: Mistress of the Dark, who had also inherited a run-down mansion. She stood beside Death who was of course dressed like The Grim Reaper he was.

Edmond, Virginia, Aria, and Bernard were also dressed as vampires. It largely looked like a Twilight convention given they were all so beautiful.

Elvis told Lawrie and I to repeat after him, and so we did. The wedding was being beamed straight from the chapel to the boulevard at Gnarly and so I knew that our wedding was also being celebrated at home.

"I now pronounce you man and wife," Elvis announced. "You may kiss the bride."

And Lawrie did. But not quite in the way I'd anticipated. I found myself in the rainforest, soaked through to the skin, as I quickly orientated myself to my new surroundings.

"A little bird told me you always wanted to be kissed in the rain like in the movies," Lawrie said, and he proceeded to do exactly that, before returning us to Vegas to sign the register and then celebrate with our guests. Vampire suggestion told Elvis we'd been there all along.

As I looked at my *husband*, and my tummy fluttered with excitement, I decided I was the luckiest girl *alive*.

Monday morning.
Nick

I looked up at the cupcake café where the object of my affections lived. One day, I hoped, now the curse was lifted, Dela might notice my existence.

Maybe this would help get her attention?

I adjusted my crane and swung the wrecking ball straight through her apartment window.

THE END

Will Nick get his Christmas wish? Find out in
SUCKING HELL.
Out December 20th. Pre-order here: https://geni.us/suckinghell
Description follows!

SUCKING HELL

All he wants for Christmas is...

Dela Francis is not convinced that the kindly, white-haired Stan A, owner of the DIY store is really Santa, even if he is shutting shop over the holiday season. 'Stan A' could just as easily be reassembled to make Satan after all.

When she discovers Stan up to devilish antics, Dela feels her suspicions might be correct.

Stan's son Nick has an unrequited crush on the fae woman who refuses to date anyone from the village. He wants Dela to see he's the one. What he needs is a Christmas miracle.

SUCKING HELL

But that seems unlikely when an escapee from the Home of the Wayward Souls threatens to spoil the festivities and the potential romance.

Can Santa save the day so that Nick and Dela can have themselves a merry little Christmas?

ABOUT ANDIE

Andie M. Long is author of the popular Supernatural Dating Agency series amongst many others.

She lives in Sheffield with her son and long-suffering partner.

When not being partner, mother, or writer, she can usually be found on Facebook or walking her whippet, Bella.

SOCIAL MEDIA LINKS

Andie's Reader Hangout on Facebook
www.facebook.com/groups/1462270007406687
(come chat books)

ABOUT ANDIE

Andie's newsletter
(get a free ebook of DATING SUCKS, a Supernatural Dating Agency prequel on sign-up)
geni.us/andiemlongparanormal

ANDIE'S OTHER PARANORMAL COMEDY BOOKS

Supernatural Dating Agency

The Vampire wants a Wife

A Devil of a Date

Hate, Date, or Mate

Here for the Seer

Didn't Sea it Coming

Phwoar and Peace

Also on audio.

Collection of Books 1-6 available.

CUPID INC
(Supernatural Dating Agency Spin-off series)

Crazy, Stupid, Lazy, Cupid

ANDIE'S OTHER PARANORMAL ROMANTIC COMEDY

Cupid and Psych

The Paranormals

Hex Factor
Heavy Souls
We Wolf Rock You
Satyrday Night Fever

Collection of all 4 books available.

Sucking Dead

Suck My Life
My Vampire Boyfriend Sucks
Sucking Hell

Made in United States
Orlando, FL
23 November 2024